Henrietta
Wellington-Green

Dominic Trelawney

Matt Khareef

Bunty Bevan

Jade Andrews

Carlos Cavello

Gilly Jumpwell

Philippa
Horsington-Charmers

Peter Fixcannon

Sam Hedges

CHAPTER ONE

An Ill Wind

January blew in with a cold blast, rattling the windows of Fetlocks Hall and howling around its draughty corridors.

Portia Manning-Smythe, headmistress of this very unusual pony school, sat huddled up in her study by a crackling log fire. So tall were the ceilings of the great Georgian house that the fire was about as effective as a candle. She was wearing a stout overcoat, a headscarf with a woolly hat on top and fingerless racing mittens. She was studying the *Racing Post*.

There were only a few days left before the winter term started and the children and their ponies would be back at school. The staff who had stayed on over Christmas to look after the resident ponies had been wonderful. One or two of the children also remained to help keep the ponies fit. Sam Hedges was one of them. She now had a second pony to ride besides her brave little Landsman. She had taken on Hob, the pony Potty Smythe (as she was known) had rescued from the ghastly Fudge family, who had been planning to sell him to the knacker man in Bristol. Hob was proving to be a brilliant event pony. Even his temperament had improved now that his previous owner had left the school.

Everybody was delighted the awful Tracy Fudge and the other two Pony Brats, Jade Andrews and Benjamin Faulkner-Fitzpain, had left Fetlocks Hall because our pony world of Terestequinus was a safer place without them. However, there was a downside to their departure.

The Pony Brats' parents had been obnoxious too but they were very rich. Their fees and patronage were now sadly missing. Andrew Fiddlit, the school accountant, had been right. Without the Pony Brats

Fetlocks Hall was struggling to survive financially. January had not only a cold wind but an ill one of numerous unpayable bills!

Refusing to skimp on the ponies' comforts, the headmistress had decided not to order any oil for the school's central heating. Sydney Sidewinder, the school caretaker, and poor old Mr Pennypot, the gardener, were sent out to cut wood which they stored in the old ice house. Sidewinder complained bitterly about having to lug it all over the house to keep the fireplaces stocked. The domestic staff needed stacks of logs to keep the fires going in the great house.

The cook, Mrs Honeybun, was instructed to buy cheaper cuts of meat for the kitchen and to shop at the low-cost cash and carry in Yeovil instead of the posh shops of Sherborne.

Ben Faloon, stable lad and brilliant shot, kept her supplied with game and Mr Pennypot had revived the old forcing house for winter vegetables.

Potty Smythe was just managing to keep the school going by the skin of its teeth until a nasty brown envelope spun through the letter box marked 'Confidential'. Groaning, she picked it up from the mat in the outer hall.

She opened it and then sank into a chair. She took

a deep breath. The letter was from a firm of solicitors called Grabbit and Screwworthy. The cheque she had written to the builders, who had fixed the crumbling ballroom roof at Fetlocks Hall, had been returned because there was simply not enough money in the bank account to cover it. They were now demanding payment in full – a rib-crunching one hundred thousand pounds!

Potty Smythe called the school accountant.

'Fiddlit,' she boomed, 'what the blazes is this? You'd better get round here straight away!'

Andrew Fiddlit sighed when he saw the letter.

'I'm sorry, Portia, dear old thing,' he frowned, 'but what did you do with the money I told you to set aside in a separate account for repairs?'

'The east wing,' sighed the headmistress.

'You should have boarded it up and let it fall down,' said Fiddlit.

'It was keeping up the rest of the school,' she returned. 'If I hadn't had the walls underpinned, Fetlocks would have slid down the hill into Middlemarsh!'

'I suppose you were relying on money from the Pony Brats' parents to get you out of this fix,' said the accountant, sitting down with his head in his hands. 'If this comes to court the judge will want to know why they took their kids out of school.'

Potty Smythe imagined trying to tell a judge and jury that three evil children, about to become A students at Fetlocks and receive certain magical powers, had left the school of their own accord – with the help of a ten-year-old girl from Milton Keynes called Penny Simms who happened to be a Unicorn Princess!

If Penny had not cleverly arranged the Pony Brats' departure, our world would have been taken over by millions of fire-breathing little red scaly Devliped ponies and their King. They had planned to seize the mythical scales, the Equilibrium of Goodness. These are always guarded by unicorns to keep the world a good place for us all to live in. If the Devlipeds had tipped the scales in the direction of evil and the unicorns lost control of them, it would have been the end to all that is fair and true!

With a story like that, the court would have sent the headmistress of Fetlocks Hall to the nearest lunatic asylum.

'How much have we got in the kitty?' asked Potty Smythe.

'Nothing,' replied Fiddlit. 'You'll have to get the bank to give you an overdraft or loan to keep the school going but that will only last you three months.

On the other hand you could sell the ancestral portraits in the refectory. They *are* by Sir Joshua Reynolds.'

Portia Manning-Smythe imagined selling the Fitznicely family portraits to unsuspecting people who would soon find out the paintings were the homes of Antonia and Arabella, Lady Sarah Fitznicely and her husband, Sir Walter, all of whom were former unicorn aristocracy and had been dead for hundreds of years. They were the resident school ghosts and would haunt wherever their pictures were hung.

'Impossible,' she said. 'But I do have some nice Dior and Norman Hartnell ball gowns from the 1950s upstairs. They may fetch something. The jewellery has all gone to the pawn shop already, I'm afraid.'

In spite of the frugal conditions in the main building the ponies continued to enjoy complete luxury in their warm stables, snuggled up deep in golden straw. Most of the ponies were clipped out, wearing three rugs each and quilted hoods, while the humans at Fetlocks were shivering miserably. The four-legged inhabitants of the school were eagerly awaiting the return of the children and their other pony friends who had gone home with them for the Christmas holidays. They were particularly looking forward to seeing their favourite little girl and Unicorn Princess, Penny Simms.

It had been four weeks since she had said goodbye to them all and they missed her terribly – especially the little skewbald pony Patch, Penny's very special friend.

You can imagine the excitement when the line of lorries, cars with trailers attached and an old red Land Rover came in through the great rusty gates and up the carriage drive to Fetlocks Hall the following Monday.

Ponies whinnied to each other, children leaned out of car or lorry windows, waving hockey sticks and jumping whips, cheering and yelling wild cries called 'view hollas' at each other, and happy parents smiled, knowing their children would have a great time back at school. Loading ramps slapped down in the stable yard. Excited ponies clattered down them, pleased to be back.

Bunty Bevan's old red Land Rover rumbled up the drive with an excited Penny Simms and various terriers on board. The Fitznicely family were waiting for her at the entrance to the park. Antonia and Arabella, looking splendid in their green velvet habits, mounted side-saddle on their chestnut ponies, galloped up to the car and sped alongside. They were joined shortly after by their lovely mother, Lady Sarah, on a handsome dapple grey and Sir Walter on his bay hunter.

'So pleased you are back at last, Princess Penny,' called Sir Walter.

'What does the speedometer read, Penny?' shouted Antonia. 'I want to know how fast Merryanzer is galloping!'

Of course nobody could see the Fitznicelys except Penny so she could only smile at them and hold a finger to her lips.

They hooted with ghostly laughter and raced away to jump the park railings and disappear into the mist.

Bunty Bevan pulled up at the foot of the stone steps leading up to the great house. Penny leapt out of the Land Rover and ran like a wild rabbit straight for the stable yard.

'Welcome back, Penny,' cried all the ponies together.

Penny stopped and curtsied to them.

'Nice to be home, ponies,' she said in their own language of Equalese, one of the magical gifts she had acquired during her test to become a Unicorn Princess.

'Penny, I'm over here!' shouted Patch.

She ran over to his stable and gave him a great hug round his brown and white neck.

'Oh, Patch! I've missed you so!' she laughed, offering him the juicy red apple she'd saved from her lunch.

'Me too,' said Patch. 'Henry and Ben have taken good care of us. Hob's turned into a really nice pony. He and Landsman have become good friends. Now Sam's got two ponies, she rides all day. She's gone team-chasing mad. It's her latest craze. Potty Smythe's hooked as well. Sam's got her to enter two teams for the Templecombe Team Chase next Saturday. We all have to gallop one and a half miles at top speed over twenty-four jumps. The fastest team wins. Sam's captain of one team and Carlos is captain of the other. She's been riding me in the afternoons or leading me off one of the others so I'm feeling pretty fit.'

'Sounds really exciting,' said Penny, who had never been team chasing in her life but knew the rules.

Just then Sam Hedges clattered into the yard on a very fit-looking Hob, leading an equally athletic Landsman.

'Hi, Pen,' she said, neatly dismounting and throwing the reins over Hob's head.

The two school chums gave each other a hug.

'Princess Penny,' said Hob, nuzzling her shoulder, 'I love you very much. If it were not for you I'd be in a tin by now!'

'And I would not have such a loyal and good friend,' added Landsman.

'You two have become real buddies,' said Penny in Equalese.

Of course Sam could not hear this conversation. It just looked as if the ponies were rubbing their noses against Penny's cheek.

'They seem to have hit it off, Sam,' she said, stroking their velvety muzzles. 'They look amazingly well.'

'Ah,' said Sam, 'there's a reason for that. We're going team chasing next Saturday. You're on Carlos's team, The Conquistadors, with Dom and Pip. There have to be four riders and ponies in a team, the fastest three through the finish to count. I'm not running with you lot because The Speed Freaks have asked me to be on their team.'

'They sound completely mad!' said Penny.

'We are,' laughed Sam. 'We were on fire last week when we won the Melbury Team Chase. We were the fastest team round over two miles and twenty-eight fences!'

'Who's on your team?' asked Penny.

'Henry's on Ned Kelly, Pat Fairbrass on Groundcover, the retrained racehorse he got from the local rehoming centre, and a new boy who's just moved into the village called Matt Khareef. He's from Dubai. His parents are dead rich. They've got oil wells or something. His dad is an Arab and his mum is from around here. They came just before Christmas to look for a school for Matt. He rides a star so I've lent him Lannie. I'm riding Hob. We're all walking the course on Friday afternoon.'

Portia Manning-Smythe was standing at the top of the steps talking to parents and trying to stop her deerhounds from chasing their dogs.

Her old chum, Bunty Bevan, came up the steps carrying Penny's small tatty suitcase. Bunty was Penny's riding instructress from Milton Keynes. It was she who had discovered Penny's talent and been instrumental in getting Penny into Fetlocks Hall. She had offered to drive Penny back to school as Mr and Mrs Simms' car was being repaired.

'Bunty, old fruit!' beamed Potty Smythe. 'Had a good trip down? Penny's on the yard already, I suppose. I heard the ponies. Come in for tea?'

The two old friends sat by the fire in the

headmistress's study with a cup of tea in one hand and a slice of fruit cake in the other.

'How's it been down here?' asked Bunty Bevan. 'Had a good Christmas, Pot?'

'Busy,' said her friend. 'Topping Boxing Day race meeting at Wincanton.'

'I went to Gilly Jumpwell's for New Year,' said Bunty. 'She still looks fabulous and rides as well as ever. She's training young riders and event horses all over the world now. She's just got back from New Zealand, lucky thing.'

'I remember her winning the European Championships years ago,' said Potty. 'Those were the days! I say, maybe I could ask her if she'd come down here and do a bit of teaching at Fetlocks.'

'She'd be expensive,' added Bunty, sipping her tea.

'I wondered if she'd do it without a fee for old times' sake,' added Potty. After all they had been top event riders together in the past. 'Trouble is, old girl, the Fetlocks piggy bank is somewhat empty since the Pony Brats left. The long and the short of it is the school's financially going down the drain. I'm being taken to court for not paying the builder for repairing the wretched ballroom roof that caved in last month. I doubt if the school will survive after this term. There's simply not enough money to run it any more. I'm afraid we will have to close down but worst of all, the ponies will have to be sold as we will not even be able to feed them!'

Bunty spluttered into her tea.

'Hell's bells, Pot,' she coughed, 'that's really sticky going! I'd help you if I had the cash. There has to be a way of saving the school. There's always our Penny. She's a resourceful child. She got us all out of a mess the last time.'

Bunty Bevan was not supposed to know about the Secret Unicorn Society (S.U.S.), but she had a pretty good idea of what it was all about. She'd guessed Penny had somehow played an important part in getting rid of the Pony Brats.

'She could be our only hope,' sighed the head-mistress.

It was a very worried Miss Bevan who finally bid her best friend goodbye and headed home for Milton Keynes. However, she was certain if anyone could save the school from being closed down and all the ponies sold off . . . it was Penny Simms.

CHAPTER TWO

Back to the Track

Once the ponies were settled in their stables, rugged up and munching their feed, the children said goodbye to their parents until half-term and made their way into the Hall.

Carlos Cavello had just returned from Brazil and found England very cold indeed. He was not prepared for the icy blasts of Fetlocks Hall with no central heating.

Philippa Horsington-Charmers, Penny's other

room-mate besides Sam Hedges, had come back from Cornwall where she had been staying with Dominic Trelawney and his family for Christmas. She, like Sam, was an orphan and had no family to go home to. Waggit, Pip's show pony, had travelled with her to Sennen in Dom's trailer with his dressage pony, Sir Fin. They were all pleased to be back. Sennen was a long way from anywhere. It was beautiful in the summer but wild and windy in the winter. Dom's parents were surfing instructors. They were both young, healthy and blond – as was their son – but not very horsey.

They lived in an old lighthouse on the edge of a cliff. The ponies were put up in the local equestrian centre, which had a big indoor arena. Dom always kept Sir Fin there as the lighthouse had no space for ponies. He could practise his dressage at the centre anyway.

Penny greeted all her friends on the way back from the yard, swapping Christmas tales and jokes. She ran up the stone steps to give her headmistress a hug but stopped on the third one between the two stone unicorns as their eyes lit up and shot out a welcoming rainbow of stars. Nobody else could see them of course except for Potty Smythe, who gave a squeal of delight.

'You see, Penny, nothing's changed,' she laughed.

Later, when things had quietened down, Princess Penny went back to the same step.

Making sure she was all alone she tapped it three times. It shot up on a hinge to reveal the hiding place of the magical gifts King Valentine Silverwings, King of the Unicorns, had given her at her coronation: the silver vial of Unicorn Tears with their healing powers, the Lance of Courage for her protection against evil, and Queen Starlight's Horn with which she could control any wild beast or monster. They were all still there.

Henry Wellington-Green, head groom at Fetlocks, bustled around the yard hanging up the ponies' rugs on the name pegs. She made sure all their tack had returned clean, arranged their grooming kits on the shelves in the tack room, and attended to any dietary requirements that might have changed in the holidays.

She was particularly pleased with herself because Peter Fixcannon, the school vet upon whom she had the most awful crush, had invited her to accompany him to the Templecombe Team Chase Ball next Saturday night. It was to be held, as was the team chasing event earlier in the day, at a huge stately home known as Templecombe Towers which belonged to the de Parrott family. They were an ancient Dorset family, whose ancestors went back to Norman days. Their enormous rambling Gothic castle was stacked with enough artefacts to rival the British Museum. Henry could hardly wait.

Ben Faloon was leaving as everybody else was arriving! He was going home to Ireland to help train racehorses for his father for the few months leading up to the Grand National, the most famous steeple-chase in the world. Willy Faloon, based in Cork, was one of the best trainers in Ireland. Ben was heading back to the track. They were all going to miss him, especially Mrs Honeybun, who had come to rely on his daily haul of rabbits, pheasants, ducks and the odd fish to supplement the financially embarrassed Fetlocks Hall menu.

Ben promised to come back to Fetlocks after the race.

Late that afternoon, Potty Smythe drove him to the airport.

'Now, Ben,' she said in confidence, 'you must be aware that we are a little short of cash up at the Hall and I'm terribly grateful for your help. I'm not a bad shot myself so I'll take the job over while you are away.

'But we've got to find a way of raising some serious cash pretty quickly or the school will have to close down. The ponies will all have to be sold. I do not know how to break it to the children. You may not have a job to come back to.'

Ben looked worried. He sat in silence for a while, deep in thought.

'Oh no, ma'am,' he said, shaking his head. 'That's not going to happen as long as the Faloons walk this earth. Can you not recruit some more rich kids with wealthy parents?'

'It's not as simple as that,' sighed Potty. 'Fetlocks children are born not made. They have to find us. I made the mistake of letting the last three bad 'uns in for the wrong reasons. On the other hand there may be one . . . He seems to tick all the right boxes and his parents are very wealthy but I've little chance of persuading them. They have the pick of all the best schools and I'm sure they will be looking for one with more academic status than Fetlocks Hall.'

Ben looked at his boots and thought again.

'There is a way I could help,' he said eventually. 'If my old horse Scudeasy would come right he could win the National with both front hoofs tied behind his back. There's a pot of money to be won and I'd give it all to the school if he was to win it. He's more than capable but for some reason known only to himself he will not race any more. Da says he's only fit to be in a tin of dog food. He'd never pay to enter him for the race and it's too expensive for me. He says the horse has some kind of mental block and should see a psychiatrist! I thought maybe I could find some kind of horse whisperer to have a chat with him to find out the problem so we could cure it.'

Potty Smythe's ears pricked up. *Who needs a horse whisperer*, she thought, *when we've got Penny?* Maybe she could have a word with Scudeasy in Equalese and find out what was wrong with him. It seemed a long shot but it might work.

The Grand National was to be run on the first Saturday in April. If the bank would lend her enough money to keep the school going until then, she could pay them back and the builders too with the prize money.

'Get him into training, Ben,' she grinned, 'and leave the rest to Aunty Potty!'

They drew up at the set-down area at the airport. Ben fetched his suitcase from the back of the Land Rover. Potty Smythe selected a rather wobbly trolley from the stack. Ben heaved his case on to it.

'I'll do my very best, ma'am,' he said with a

sideways smile and a twinkle in his eye.

'Ring me as soon as you get home,' said the headmistress. 'Let me know what Willy thinks and I'll have a word with him. I know he trusts me.'

With that they shook hands and Ben strode off with the trolley towards the check-in area.

Portia Manning-Smythe swung away into the twilight and headed back to Fetlocks Hall.

CHAPTER THREE

The Templecombe Chase

The next day Potty Smythe telephoned her old chum Gilly Jumpwell to ask if she might have a week spare to come down to Dorset from Leicestershire to give some lessons on horse trialling or eventing. Gilly was the best instructress in the world for this demanding sport. It involved the three disciplines of dressage, cross-country riding and showjumping. You needed a very special pony to do this as he had to be calm, courageous and athletic all at the same time. Potty thought Penny in particular would make a brilliant eventer but was not sure that Patch would be able to do the dressage section quite so well. He had rather short legs and did not possess the floating paces of a dressage pony like Sir Fin. However, he jumped well and was very brave.

Portia Manning-Smythe explained that she was unable to pay Gilly but she did have a spare ticket for the Team Chase Ball at Templecombe the following Saturday worth one hundred and fifty pounds. This included a seat on the Masters' Table, a cracking meal and dancing all night to the Black and Blues Band, toast of the south-west.

Gilly accepted and said she'd be down on Saturday evening. As a favour to her old chum she agreed to give the Fetlocks children some event training, starting on the Tuesday after the ball. She planned the lessons to last for three days, culminating in a real one-day event competition on the fourth day.

It was Friday, the day before the chase. The two teams jumped into the back of Potty Smythe's Land Rover and set off for Templecombe to walk the course. Matt Khareef was going to meet them there at two o'clock.

They rumbled through the gate of a big flat field to the east of the castle. Potty parked up by the secretary's caravan. There was a plan of the course pinned up in the window.

'Looks straightforward enough,' said Henry, who was pathfinder or leader on Ned for The Speed Freaks. Carlos agreed. He was pathfinder for The Conquistadors and had borrowed a really fast horse called Charlotte Allstar from Peter Fixcannon, the vet. She was not a particularly easy ride, with no brakes at all. She was very bold and took every fence in her stride. It was pretty pointless even trying to stop her and you needed Carlos's nerves of steel to ride her!

A very smart black four-wheel drive pulled up alongside the Land Rover. The door opened and a tall dark-skinned man got out, followed by a small boy.

'Hi, Matt. Hello, Mr Khareef,' shouted Sam, running over to the boy and his father. 'Come and meet our other team.'

Penny could not help noticing how small Matt was. He was twelve years old but was even shorter than she was at ten. He had huge dark eyes like his father and the same shock of jet black hair but none of his height. His skin was obviously brown but much paler than his dad's.

'His mum must be tiny,' she smiled to herself.

Matt shook hands with everybody. He seemed very nice and dead keen on ponies.

Penny liked him straight away.

'It is very kind of Sam to lend Matt her horse,' said Mr Khareef to Potty Smythe.

'She would not have even dreamt of lending her precious Landsman to anyone who could not ride like a star,' said Potty, 'and Matt is certainly very talented.'

Potty was secretly hoping that Mr and Mrs Khareef would send their tiny son to Fetlocks but she knew they were looking at other schools in the area. She didn't want to put them off by being too pushy as she knew people like the Khareefs would not appreciate it. She thought it best to keep quiet and see how things developed.

They all marched off towards the first fence, a small log with a pole for a ground line. The course was one and a quarter miles long over twenty-eight fences. The jumps started off reasonably small but increased in size and difficulty all the way round until you reached a 'collecting' fence, which involved jumping over a rail into a farmyard. Here the pathfinder, or whichever horse was in the lead by then, had to wait until the rest of the team had caught up with him in the yard. Once all members were collected, the leader could then proceed by jumping out of the farmyard over another rail. Then they ran on over ten more jumps, including a drop fence into a pond, before finishing over a monster-sized hedge with a double rail in it.

Mr Khareef strode along beside Portia Manning-Smythe, obviously struck by the way she was instructing the teams about how to ride each fence.

In fact Potty had her fingers crossed all the way round the course. She desperately wanted to impress Mr Khareef. The Khareefs were fantastically rich. If she was lucky enough to get them to send Matt to Fetlocks they would become patrons. This would mean sponsoring the school to some extent. It would certainly help with the problems looming on the horizon.

'Just be sure you know your course, everybody,' said Potty, 'especially you pathfinders. If you get left behind just follow the hoof prints of the other horses. There's a dangerous quarry a few fields away called Magilly's Pit. You don't want to go anywhere near that place if you can help it.'

Matt was really excited to be running with The Speed Freaks again.

'We'll win tomorrow!' he shouted, waving good-bye as the black four-wheel drive swished over the turf towards the road.

The Fetlocks children chattered non-stop on the way home. They all seemed full of confidence except Pip, who was not sure about Waggit's ability to jump the third fence, a swollen brook at the bottom of a meadow, let alone the drop fence into the pond.

'Oh, just kick on and tuck in behind me,' said Dom, squeezing her hand.

The rest of the afternoon and evening was spent getting the horses and ponies ready. They were shampooed and plaited ready for the morning. The tack was cleaned until it gleamed. Bandages, rugs, buckets and sponges, water containers, first-aid kit and riding clothes complete with back protectors and the teams' new sweatshirts were loaded into the lorry. Mrs Honeybun had made the best picnic lunch she could, including a large fruit cake with almond and cherry topping.

After supper everyone went to bed huddled up with blankets and hot-water bottles. The only inhabitants of Fetlocks Hall not shivering all night were the Fitznicely family, who were waiting to say goodnight to Penny at the top of the stairs.

'The cold does not affect us, dear sister Penny,' giggled Arabella, screwing off her head and tucking it under her arm. 'We have been dead for years and are as cold as the grave!'

'I do wish you wouldn't do that, Bella,' said Penny. 'It is really disgusting.'

'We've been getting our ponies fit for the team chase tomorrow,' said Antonia.

'Yes, we'll be running as well,' added Sir Walter.

'We have named our team The Fast Phantoms,' smiled Lady Sarah.

'Well, you'll be hard to catch,' said Penny. 'Merry was doing thirty miles an hour the other day by the Land Rover speedometer!'

Saturday morning came in with a great deal of fog.

Patch was so excited about the forthcoming chase that he did not eat his breakfast. He and the other Fetlocks ponies stood wearing their travel boots, tail guards and rugs, waiting to be loaded into the two school horseboxes.

Henry led Ned Kelly, her former racehorse, up the ramp, followed by Patch, Hob and Landsman. Waggit, Pip's pretty grey pony, was to travel in the other lorry, driven by Pat Fairbrass, with

Groundcover and Budget, the pony Dom had borrowed from the school. His own pony, Sir Fin, was not allowed to go team chasing in case he hurt himself. Being the junior dressage pony of the year, he was too valuable to risk at a dangerous sport like that. Peter Fixcannon had arranged to bring Charlotte Allstar to the event in his own lorry for Carlos.

They arrived at Templecombe at ten thirty. The lorries were being directed to the old kennels a quarter of a mile from the great Gothic castle with its spooky towers pointing skyward over the treetops. They had to get a move on to arrive at the event by eleven o'clock.

Penny was delighted to see the Fitznicely family there. Of course no one else could see them except her, Potty Smythe and the ponies. Antonia and Arabella, wearing matching green velvet side-saddle habits and small neat hats, each with a short russet-coloured feather and veil, were seated on their two matching chestnut ponies. Their mother, Lady Sarah, looked stunning in a dark blue velvet habit trailing almost to the ground, with lace stock and white doe-skin gloves. She wore a tricorne hat with a black feather. Her long blonde ringlets were swept back and tied with a black bow. She was seated, side-saddle, on a dapple grey mare that looked very much like an Arabian cross thoroughbred. Her elderly husband, Sir Walter, was wearing a military-style coat of the same colour with gold brocade, a similar hat, buff-coloured breeches and long black boots. He rode his bay hunter, Maldoon, who had a very short tail.

They looked so incredible that Penny thought it a shame that they were ghosts and none of her team-mates could see them.

'Hello, Penny,' said the twins as the whole family trotted up to the lorry.

'Where are the de Parrotts?' said Lady Sarah. 'This is their party and they aren't out yet.'

Just then another ghostly family floated out from the castle stable yard and galloped over the fields towards their relatives, passing straight through a row of lorries.

There were three boys from about ten to seventeen years of age, all dressed in eighteenth-century riding clothes on short-tailed ponies. Their parents, impeccably turned out in similar style to the Fitznicelys, were in maroon velvet with silver buttons. Lady Beatrice de Parrott was riding a brown horse, similar in breed to Lady Sarah's. Sir Rupert de Parrott was on a black hunter with a very fine head.

'Hello, sister dear,' said Lady Sarah to Lady Beatrice. Sir Walter dashingly took off his hat to his sister-in-law. Sir Rupert did the same.

'I'd like you to meet Her Royal Highness Penelope, reigning Unicorn Princess. She has recently joined our family.'

The de Parrotts welcomed Penny and wished her team the best of luck.

'Oh, do run along now, dear,' said Sir Walter. 'Your people are calling you over to get your pony ready.'

'What strange coloured ponies the children ride these days,' commented Michael de Parrott, their eldest son and something of a fop, as Penny led Patch down the ramp.

'Did you see those ghosts, Patch?' asked Penny.

'Of course,' he said. 'Ponies can see ghosts but we can't understand much of what they say unless they are former unicorn royalty because ordinary ghosts can't speak Equalese. The Fitznicelys often come out haunting on horseback. It's the de Parrotts' idea to have this team chase today. They are giving the Ball tonight.'

Penny felt comforted that ponies could see ghosts as it was another thing she had in common with them.

'Hooray!' said Patch. 'Here's Charlotte arriving in the vet's lorry. We're all here now, so let's go, Penny!'

The two teams, mounted on their ponies, crowded around Potty Smythe for a final briefing before heading down to the start.

The Speed Freaks were the third team to go out of thirty teams. The Conquistadors were following straight after them.

Penny was just wondering about The Fast Phantoms when Bella and Antonia shot past her in their side-saddles towards the practice jump.

'We are running last,' shouted Bella over her shoulder. 'We don't want to be slowed down by any of you live slugs!'

'The de Parrotts are fifteenth to go but those boys and their father will be no match for us!' cried Antonia.

Penny had no time to reply. The Speed Freaks were lining up ready for the starter's flag. Her team would be running in five minutes so there was just time to pop Patch over the practice jump behind the others.

Henry was already leading her team at top speed towards the first jump, closely followed by Pat, then Sam and Matt on their excited horses.

Although Penny was a very brave rider she had never taken part in a team chase before and she did feel a few butterflies batting around in her tummy as The Conquistadors lined up for the start.

Patch was eager to go and danced up and down on his little hoofs.

'Come on, everybody,' shouted Carlos. 'Line up behind me. You know the order – me first, then Dom, Pip, and Penny last.'

'One minute to go, Conquistadors,' yelled the starter. 'I'll count you down.'

Penny forgot her butterflies as she stroked Patch's brown and white neck, reassuring him everything would be all right.

'Five, four, three, two, one, GO!' shouted the man at the start line as his flag came down and Carlos shot forward on Charlotte Allstar. The four of them were soon galloping up to the first fence.

'*Wheee!* That was easy!' breathed Patch as he sailed over it.

'Don't pull so hard,' said Penny as they sped down to the next jump. 'We've got a long way to go and you mustn't run out of puff!'

Pip and Waggit nipped smartly over a thick hedge just in front of them and they galloped off down the meadow to the brook.

Dom glanced over his shoulder.

'Come on, Pip,' he yelled. 'Get on my tail for this one!'

Pip kicked Waggit on and came alongside Dom and Budget. Penny, splattered with mud, could not hold Patch now. She shot past both of them.

Carlos and Charlotte leapt the brook, closely followed by Penny and Patch.

Dom and Budget flew over but Waggit, who did not like getting his feet wet at the best of times, stuck his toes in on the bank and came to an abrupt halt. Pip went sailing over his head. There was a loud splash as she hit the muddy water.

Carlos and Penny were not aware of the accident until Penny looked over her right shoulder and saw Waggit galloping madly, riderless and alone, on the other side of the hedge heading towards the quarry!

She screamed at Carlos to stop but he could not hold Charlotte and they disappeared over a big hedge with a ditch in front of it.

Dom had heard the splash and stopped Budget. He immediately raced back to the brook and jumped off to rescue Pip.

He plunged waist deep into the water and fished her out.

'I should have brought my board!' he laughed, hauling her on to the bank.

Pip was more concerned about Waggit, who had run off through a gateway in the hedgerow. Penny had galloped back to the scene of the accident. She pulled Patch up and trotted back to the water's edge.

'I'll get Waggit,' she reassured her friends and set off through the gateway in pursuit of the little grey pony.

Poor Waggit was now lost and frightened. He was running blindly towards the dangerous quarry, Magilly's Pit, unaware that he could fall in.

He was three fields away by now and Penny had no way of catching him up. There was no alternative. She was going to have to use the Equibatic skills she had been given as a Unicorn Princess to rescue Waggit.

'*Let's Fly*, Patch,' she said.

The little pony lifted off the ground and flew easily over three fields and hedges.

Patch was nearly level with Waggit but the quarry was only about fifty metres away.

'Come on, boy!' breathed Penny as she urged Patch down. 'Keep your feet up off the ground. I'm going to have to grab him and take him up with us or he will be killed! Whoa, Waggit! Steady, little boy,' she said to the bolting pony in Equalese. But he was too frightened to hear.

Five metres to go! Patch was flying level with Waggit now, his feet tucked up.

Just as the ground disappeared from beneath them, Penny grabbed the grey pony's reins and shouted, '*Let's Fly!*'

Both ponies soared into the air. Magilly's Pit disappeared below them.

Waggit was saved.

Penny circled both ponies in the air. Waggit had never flown before and was having a great time.

'How did you do that?' he asked.

'Don't ask daft questions,' said Patch. 'She's a Unicorn Princess and she can do anything. How do you think she understands what we are saying, you silly pony, and why did you stop at that little brook anyway?'

Penny could see Dom and Pip below but of course they could not see her because she and the ponies were invisible when flying.

She landed Waggit and Patch in the field behind the hedge, close to where Waggit had made a quick escape through the gateway earlier. She trotted neatly through the gap, leading Waggit. Dom had taken off his sweater and wrapped it around Pip to keep her warm. She was soaking wet, right through to her knickers. It was a cold day and she was shivering.

She brightened up when she saw Penny trotting up with her beloved pony in tow.

They all turned round at the sound of a quad bike coming towards them across the fields.

It was driven by Potty Smythe with Carlos by her side and Henry hanging on to the seat behind.

'What happened to you lot?' shouted Potty Smythe. 'Are you OK, Pip?'

'I had a fall at the brook,' said Pip, 'but I'm just wet. No bones broken.'

'Oh, is that all?' laughed Henry, who was almost completely covered in farmyard slurry. She had come off Ned over a big fence and landed in a very smelly ditch near the end of the course. Bravely, she had managed to get back on and complete the course, bringing her team home to win the event.

Penny knew Henry thought The Conquistadors were softies for giving up the chase and coming home. She would love to say, 'Well, actually, Patch and I became invisible and flew through the air to rescue Waggit from plunging down a ghastly quarry. We saved his life.' But that was Secret Unicorn Society business and highly secret.

Portia Manning-Smythe gave her a wink. She had

36

not seen the accident but had a feeling that once again Penny had been in the right place at the right time.

The teams were back at the lorries getting the ponies dried off and ready to return to Fetlocks when the triumphant Fast Phantoms trotted past.

'We won of course!' shouted Antonia. 'We were ten seconds faster than your Speed Freaks. Pity your lot could not see our round.'

'Nice work at the quarry, Penny,' said Lady Sarah. 'You are more than worthy to be a Unicorn Princess, young lady.'

'Fantastic Equibatics,' added Sir Walter. 'Best flying I've ever seen.'

Of course nobody else knew that The Fast Phantoms were the real winners of the team chase except Penny and Potty Smythe and the ponies. It would have been a bit difficult to explain to the very cock-a-hoop Speed Freaks that they'd just been beaten by a team who had been dead for years!

The two school lorries rumbled out over the rutted field towards the road. A big shiny trophy was lying on the dashboard of one of them and the windscreen was sporting four large red rosettes hanging on a line of baler twine. Sam, Matt, Pat and

Henry were reliving every moment of their prize-winning round to the others.

Henry was anxious to get the children and their ponies safely home and put to bed. She had to leg it back to her cottage and get cleaned up as soon as possible. They were all teasing her about how awful she smelt after her swim in that slurry ditch. Peter Fixcannon, the vet, was picking her up at seven o'clock for the Team Chase Ball. It had been a big day for her but this was going to be an even bigger night!

CHAPTER FOUR

The Ball

At 6 p.m. on Saturday, the evening of the ball, a blue sports car purred up to the front steps of Fetlocks Hall.

Gilly Jumpwell swung her long slim legs out of the car and made her way up to the house.

'Gilly! Darling girl!' shouted Potty Smythe. 'My goodness, you don't look a day older than thirty. How do you do it?' In fact Gilly was nearly twice that age but with her New Zealand tan, blonde hair, ice-blue eyes and perfect nails she certainly did not look it.

Under her elegant evening coat she was wearing a long sea-blue chiffon ball gown with a very low back and a fishtail. It showed off her perfect figure. Portia Manning-Smythe, who had never had a perfect figure in her life, was wearing a long black velvet skirt with matching loose top decorated with sparkling beads. It would have been nice to still own the diamond necklace and earrings that once went with it but they had been pawned earlier to pay the last feed bill and the farrier.

The two old friends gave each other a hug. Potty walked Gilly into the house, passing the Fitznicelys who were also getting ready for the ball.

'Oh, Mama,' said the twins. 'You look so beautiful!'

Lady Sarah floated down the stairs in the latest fashion of her day, a French silk brocade ball gown in rose-petal pink, expertly styled hair studded with pearls, long white gloves and pink pearl necklace. Sir Walter, in white wig, thigh-length cream silk jacket with gold brocade and buttons, white breeches, stockings and pumps, looked her perfect escort.

'Oh, Papa,' said Antonia. 'You will be the most handsome man at the ball. We think it is such a bad business that we have to stay behind in our portraits. Can we not come too and watch from the stairs with our Templecombe cousins?'

'Oh, all right then,' said Sir Walter, giving in, 'but you will have to promise to be very good. No noisy haunting around the castle to frighten the guests.'

Antonia and Arabella squealed with delight and clapped their little ghostly hands.

'And can we bring our sister, Princess Penelope?'

'That's going to be difficult. People will be able to see her but not you,' said Lady Sarah. 'I do not know how she will get there. She cannot just materialise like us unless she's Equibatic.'

'Then she shall come on her pony,' said the twins and they floated off to find Penny.

Henry was in a flap! It was half past six and her hair was a mess. She had only returned from the yard half an hour before, had a quick shower and scrubbed away the remains of the smelly slurry she was covered in after her fall into the ditch. She tried to twist her long dark hair up into a French roll but it just would not perform. She squirted some extra-hold mousse on it, hung her hair upside down and dried it. When she stood up it looked as if she had had an electric shock!

She washed it all over again to get the stuff out.

The doorbell went.

'Oh NO,' she screamed. Her dream prince, Peter Fixcannon MRCVS, was at the door and she was in her dressing gown with soaking wet hair!'

She peevishly opened the door and peered round it.

'You look fabulous!' laughed the vet. 'Good round, wasn't it?'

She apologised, opened the door, and he marched in carrying a corsage of orchids.

Henry did have a nice ball gown. It had just come back from the cleaners and was still in its plastic bag. It was a peacock-green strapless taffeta prom dress with a nipped-in waist. Somewhere there was a handbag to match and very high-heeled shoes. Henry rummaged around in her untidy bedroom for them.

Her heart sank when she realised she had left her make-up bag in the lorry back at Fetlocks! It was too late to go and fetch it now. She only had some of her mother's very pale powder and an ancient bright red lipstick. She thought she looked very strange in it but there was no time to take it all off and start again. She found the shoes and handbag and glanced at herself in the mirror.

Peter Fixcannon's former girlfriend, the beautiful, rich Lavinia Darling, would have had an expensive hairdo, stunning dress and perfect make-up. She had left the team chase earlier, handing her dapple grey mare to her groom and stepping into her father's chauffeur-driven Rolls-Royce. *She* did not have to stay until the end of the event, get all the children and ponies home, make sure the ponies were washed off, dried, checked for injuries, rugged up and fed, the tack cleaned and the horseboxes mucked out, and finally run around the yard to check that the other ponies were tucked up for the night!

'Come on, Henry, we'll be late for our table,' called Peter Fixcannon.

Henry took a deep breath, opened her bedroom door and just stood there.

'Stunning!' said Peter. 'Love the arty make-up! Gorgeous dress. The colour really suits you.' He helped fix her hair with a silver clasp and pinned the orchids into it.

Henry beamed. He really was the dearest man. He removed the cleaning ticket from the back of the green dress and held her coat as she slid her arms into the sleeves. Once outside, he opened the car door for her and away they went to the ball.

Potty Smythe and Gilly Jumpwell were picked up

by a minibus which they had hired along with some people from the other teams.

It was full of jolly people, all looking forward to a good night out. Anthony Redcheek, the team captain of The Magnificent Mayos, was quite smitten with Gilly and asked if he could engage her for a dance later on.

Templecombe had a massive dining hall and ball-room. There was no need to put up a marquee. The guests were arriving in droves. Some of the gentle-men were dressed in red tailcoats with dark blue collars and black trousers. Most of the ladies looked wonderful except for the odd one or two who had tried to squeeze themselves into dresses two sizes too small for them. Gilly Jumpwell winced as a fat blubbery woman pushed past her in a tight strapless dress.

Ant Redcheek handed Gilly a glass of champagne. He was not the only gentleman to notice her. She was certainly turning s   heads, both dead and alive. Even Sir Walter smiled and bowed at her.

'Ah ha!' said Lady Sarah from behind her fan to her sister Lady Beatrice. 'Did you see that?'

'It's well her living admirers cannot see us, dear heart,' said Lady Beatrice. 'Their heads would swivel right off!'

Both ghostly beauties giggled and turned towards the ballroom doors.

'Oh, do look, there's old Count Blackdrax come in with Fern Montecute. His gout is worse than ever and he has more warts upon his face than fleas in his wig! What does she see in him?'

'A large estate in Hampshire and a tea fortune,' whispered her sister. They giggled even more and walked, arm in arm, straight through a wall into the drawing room.

Back at Fetlocks Hall, Penny was doing her homework alone in the library when Arabella and Antonia floated in.

'Guess what?' said Antonia. 'Mother and Father have already left to haunt the ball and the three of us are being allowed to watch.'

Penny told them off for teasing her but they soon persuaded her that she would be coming with them according to their plan.

'As you ain't dead yet,' said Arabella, 'you cannot haunt. We can and it's great fun scaring the pantaloons off live people. We simply appear and disappear whenever we want.' Arabella demonstrated her point by suddenly appearing on a somewhat dusty chandelier far above Penny. In a flash she reappeared by her side.

'This is a good one,' said Antonia, sticking her tongue out. It became so long it reached the hem of her dress.

'That's disgusting!' cried Penny. 'Even when I'm as dead as you I'll never do such a thing!'

'Not as bad as this one,' hooted Arabella in a mock ghostly voice. She pulled off her left hand with her right one and set it on the table where it crawled along all on its own.

'Yuck!' said Penny.

'We are out for some fun tonight,' said Antonia. 'Oh, do come, Penny. It will be such a laugh. You are invisible when you are Equibatic so people won't see you. Now go and get Patch from his stable and fly on over to Templecombe. We'll meet you outside by the fountain on the carriage drive, just in front of the main entrance.

Patch was asleep, snoring in deep golden straw. He was tired after his day's team chasing.

Penny stole down to the stable yard around 8 p.m. She unlocked the tack room and took his bridle off its peg. Henry, Potty and the other grown-ups had already left so the coast was clear.

Patch was surprised to see Penny at that time of

the night. When she told him what she wanted him to do, he simply snorted and rolled over.

'Oh, come on, Patch,' she whispered. 'You can do it. You told me how fit you are.'

Eventually he agreed but it took a lot of persuading and packets of mint treats. He pulled himself to his feet.

'I'm only doing this because I love you, Penny,' he yawned.

She gave him a hug and put his bridle on.

Soon they were flying over the treetops towards Templecombe.

The castle looked even spookier from above with its Gothic towers pointing up at them. It was a blaze of light. All the floodlights were on around the castle and grounds so it was easy to find from the sky.

Penny circled Patch over the front drive. Below her was a huge fountain with leaping mer-horses branching out from it. They looked beautiful in the floodlights, water spurting from their open mouths. Antonia and Arabella were sitting on two of them, waving up at Penny.

'Don't let Patch's feet touch the ground, Penny,' they shouted, 'or you will stop being invisible to the live people.'

Patch groaned. Hovering was tiring and he did not

know how long he could keep it up.

'Give us a lift,' called the ghostly little girls, beckoning to Penny.

She made Patch hover above the fountain. The twins instantly appeared seated behind her. As they did not weigh anything Patch had no trouble flying through the castle's great doors and up the staircase to where the de Parrott children were waiting.

'Fantastic!' said James de Parrott, ten-year-old son of Lady Beatrice and Sir Rupert.

'Glad you could come too, Princess Penny,' said his brother Sebastian, who was twelve. He bowed and kissed her hand as she sat on Patch.

'Michael's gone with Mama and Papa. He's seventeen so he's allowed to go to balls. He's infatuated with Fern Montecute, you know, but her family are marrying her off to that old brute, Count Blackdrax!'

'Why does the count haunt round here so much?' asked Antonia.

'There's a picture of him somewhere in the cellar at Fetlocks Hall. It's a drawing by Isaac Cruikshank. He likes it so he hangs out in it when he isn't haunting Blackdrax Castle in Hampshire,' said Sebastian.

'If we are to do some fun haunts tonight,' said Arabella, 'we will have to make sure the parents and Aunt Portia don't see us because we have promised to be on our best behaviour.'

'We'll be careful,' said the boys.

'Look, there's a live one coming out of the dining hall,' whispered Arabella. 'Let's go for it! Watch this, Princess Penny.'

Gilly Jumpwell was looking for the cloakroom. It was down a long dark corridor which was ideal for haunting. She swished across the hall, still holding her champagne glass.

Penny watched Arabella take the glass out of her hand.

To Gilly it simply disappeared. She stopped, looked curiously at her hand, glanced at the floor, shook her head and carried on.

Penny, still hovering on Patch, went into fits of giggles.

Gilly carried on along the dark corridor. The ghostly flock of children, Penny and Patch floated after her.

She entered the smallest room, followed by Antonia. When she swished back across the great hall she was unknowingly trailing a complete roll of loo paper behind her that Antonia had stuck into her knickers!

Penny and the ghosts all hooted with laughter. This ghostly giggle did not go unnoticed by a maid who was coming up from the kitchens with a tray of jelly. She screamed and dropped it. One of the butlers, who had been following closely behind her with a tray of silver creamers, slipped in the jelly and covered himself in cream!

The children had to stifle another peal of ghostly laughter. Patch was laughing too. He was having a great time.

Ant Redcheek, all eyes on Gilly, saw his chance. He gallantly stepped up behind her and stood on the trailing loo paper before too many people saw it. He gathered it up as she stopped and turned round to meet his eyes.

'Anthony Redcheek, at your service, madam,' he grinned. 'You dropped this?' He stuffed the loo paper into a nearby urn.

Gilly beamed. 'Seem to have lost my drink as well,' she said.

'Allow me to get you another,' smiled Ant.

Just then the dinner gong was sounded and they moved off with the other guests towards the great banqueting hall.

After grace was said by Sir Edwin de Parrott, the current titleholder, all the guests sat down to a sumptuous four-course meal.

The ghostly families had their own menu of course, which was even more sumptuous and consisted of eight courses and a great deal more wine.

Count Blackdrax had dribbled jus of cranberry and wild boar down his cravat. His wig had slipped back so he resembled a pig himself.

The lovely sixteen-year-old Fern Montecute seated at his side was most embarrassed.

James de Parrott, careful not to be seen by any other ghosts, crawled under the table and pulled the tail of the old count's wig. It fell off to reveal his horrid bald head complete with purple carbuncle. But Count Blackdrax was too quick for James. He reached down and grabbed him by the scruff of his collar.

'Little ruffian!' he raged, hauling James upright. 'I'll take my stick to you!'

Fern stepped in. 'Come, come, my lord,' she smiled prettily, ''tis but a childish prank. I will take him to his brother.'

Old Count Blackdrax spluttered a grin, showing his blackened teeth.

'As you wish, my dear,' he grimaced, handing James over to Fern.

Michael de Parrott asked to be excused from his table and vanished out on to the terrace to meet

Fern, who had drifted out with James in tow.

Fern scolded James and told him to reappear with the group of children who were now back at the top of the stairs above the great hall, and looking as if butter would not melt in their spooky little mouths.

After dinner the band struck up.

The Black and Blues band played funky blues music, rock and roll classics, pop, hip hop and anything the dancers requested. They were very versatile and really good.

The ghostly dancers had their own music and dancing in the great drawing room at Templecombe. However, some of the more adventurous ones preferred to stay in the ballroom and have a go at modern dance with the Black and Blues.

This was quite something to see. It seemed that Potty Smythe was jiving on her own to some very crazy rock and roll. She'd grown up in the 1950s so she was very good at it although a little stiff these days. In fact she was not alone at all, but was trying to teach Sir Walter Fitznicely to jive!

'Oh, do let's dance!' said Sebastian and they all joined in. Penny and Patch had a chance to show off their Equiballet, which delighted all the ghosts. As they danced above the crowd in perfect time to the music Potty Smythe, who was the only one who could see them, slipped Penny a wink.

Patch, although he was enjoying the ball immensely, was now tiring rapidly. It was nearly midnight and he'd been hovering or flying for four hours. He'd also been team chasing all day.

It really was time to go home.

Penny thanked the others for inviting her to the ball and waved goodbye as she left them far below on the lawn at Templecombe.

'That was awesome!' said Patch as they flew back to Fetlocks.

'You were brilliant,' said Penny, flinging her arms round his neck as they spun away into the moonlight.

CHAPTER FIVE

The Ugly Picture

Henry plodded around the stable yard at 7 a.m. the morning after the ball.

She had been dancing until 4 a.m. and did not feel like work at all. But ponies always come first and they had to be fed and turned out in their winter rugs, the stables mucked out and the usual everyday routine of Fetlocks Hall completed. Patch was still asleep. She wondered if he was all right, so instead of just clipping his feed bucket on to his door in the usual way, she came in and walked over to him. He suddenly woke up, glanced at her, then heaved himself up on to his four feet. He stretched and yawned, before strolling over for his feed.

'Poor Patch,' said Henry. 'You did have a hard day's work yesterday, didn't you?'

Little did she know that Penny and Patch had been boogieing above her and Peter Fixcannon last night.

Penny and the other children were busying themselves with their yard duties before breakfast.

In the headmistress's study Potty Smythe was on the telephone to Ben Faloon in Ireland.

'I've persuaded Da to let me run old Scudeasy in the Grand National,' he told her, 'but he can't spare a jockey so I'll have to ride him myself. He's had a couple of days' practice out over our training fences and enjoyed himself but he's still as slow as an old goat when running against the other horses.'

'What are his chances of winning?' asked Potty Smythe, sipping black coffee.

'A hundred to one for sure, if he stays miles ahead of the pack. But that is almost impossible,' said Ben. 'Da still says he'd be better off sending him to the knacker man if he doesn't improve. Have you managed to find any rich new pupils yet?'

'Not really,' sighed the headmistress. 'There is a

possibility but that's a hundred to one shot as well!'

Potty Smythe groaned. There were only a couple of months before the big race at Aintree and there was little chance of Scudeasy winning it. However, a lifetime with horses had taught her that they always have a reason for behaving in strange ways. It was just a matter of finding out what objection Scudeasy had to galloping with other horses.

Her plan was to make a trip to Cork, taking Penny with her. She knew the unicorns had given the little girl the power to speak Equalese so she was hoping Penny could ask Scudeasy why he had such a problem with racing. If there was a solution she might be able to cure it. On the other hand, if he was simply refusing to cooperate, Penny might get some results by politely asking him if he wouldn't mind trying at Aintree just this once as the future of Fetlocks Hall depended on it. That meant she was going to have to tell Penny all about the trouble Fetlocks was in.

The next day, Potty sent for her after lunch and told her the whole story.

Penny was horrified that the law courts might close the school down because of debt and send in bailiffs to take the ponies away to be sold. She shuddered at the thought of any of them, especially her darling Patch, being sent to Exeter market where the knacker men would be bidding for ponies for meat. She racked her brains to try to think of a way of helping the school. Ben and Scudeasy simply had to win this great race. Everything depended on it.

'King Valentine Silverwings gave you the power to speak to horses and ponies,' said Potty Smythe. 'Perhaps you could ask Scudeasy what he finds so difficult about racing other horses. If we can find out what the problem is and put it right, there is every chance he will win the race.'

Penny thought for a moment.

'I have never tried horse psychiatry before,' she mused, 'but I am willing to have a go if it will save Fetlocks and keep Scudeasy out of a tin.'

'That's my girl!' said Potty Smythe.

Gilly Jumpwell was looking forward to giving the children some lessons in horse trialling. They did not start until Tuesday so on Monday morning she went to an auction of Sporting Art at the sale rooms in Sherborne. Secretly, she was also meeting Anthony Redcheek for lunch at The Huntsman's Tap. She had left the sale catalogue behind on the occasional table outside the headmistress's study. It caught Penny's eye as she was leaving the room after her talk with Potty Smythe.

She recognised something about the picture on the front cover. It was a very old picture of Count Blackdrax, whom she had seen at the ball. He was seated, looking quite repulsive, on a very ugly horse.

She read the details of the picture offered for sale.

'Seventeenth-century mezzotint print of the notorious Count Blackdrax by Isaac Cruikshank, circa 1776. Expected to fetch in the region of ten thousand pounds.'

Her heart leapt! She remembered Sebastian mentioning that the old count often haunted a picture of himself by the same artist somewhere in the cellar at Fetlocks Hall. If the one in the catalogue was just a print and being sold for ten thousand pounds, what was the original drawing worth?

She made up her mind to find it. She had not liked the look of Count Blackdrax. If he was haunting the cellar, she was not going down there alone or unarmed.

She decided to tell the Fitznicely family about her plan to find Count Blackdrax's picture.

Sir Walter had previously told her that if she ever needed their help she should twist the wooden unicorn on the banisters at the bottom of the stairs. That night around midnight, when Fetlocks Hall was still, she did exactly that.

The Fitznicely family came floating down from their portraits in the refectory. They were still recovering from Saturday night's ball so looked a little dishevelled.

She told them about the money problems the school was experiencing and how it was vital to raise some cash to save it. She explained her plan to find Count Blackdrax's portrait as it was worth a lot of money and could be sold to help keep Fetlocks Hall going. At the mention of finding and selling Blackdrax's picture they all looked a little worried.

'It's not as if he hasn't got anywhere else to go,' said Lady Sarah. 'He's got loads more portraits to haunt at Blackdrax Castle and a simply ghastly one hanging in Dorchester museum.'

'He's a mean old devil though,' said Sir Walter. 'He's not going to give it up easily. He haunts it when he comes over to visit Fern, his betrothed, at Montecute House. It's not far away from here.'

'That's the answer,' said Antonia. 'He'd do anything for Fern and she'd do anything for cousin Michael. Maybe we could get Michael to ask Fern to persuade the old warthog to vacate the Fetlocks Hall picture and haunt the one in the museum in Dorchester instead. After all, the museum's about the same distance from Montecute House as here so he won't have far to float.'

'Oh, my dear sister,' cried Arabella, 'you are genius itself!'

Michael de Parrott was so in love with Fern Montecute that the thought of her having to marry old Count Blackdrax made his blood boil. She was so much younger than him and in an ordinary lifetime he would have died soon and left her a very rich widow.

However, being dead already there was no chance of this and Fern would be joined to the ugly old carbuncle for immortality. Michael stood no chance. Lord and Lady Montecute were dead set on the marriage with the count because Montecute was a very large estate and expensive to run. The settlement offered by Count Blackdrax for their beautiful daughter's hand in marriage would keep it going.

Fern was in love with Michael but she did not approve of his foppish ways. He was a snappy dresser and spent his ghostly allowance from his parents investing in silly inventions thought up by other young ghosts like himself. The Montecutes disapproved of him and felt sorry for his parents.

Michael was more than happy to ask Fern to persuade the count to give up his haunting place to help his uncle, aunt and cousins Fitznicely retain theirs. Fetlocks Hall was their home. If it was sold and the bailiffs took their portraits the Fitznicelys would have to move with them.

The Fitznicelys told Penny to leave it up to them. They would have the Montecutes and the de Parrotts over for dinner at Fetlocks to give Michael a chance to put the idea to Fern.

There was great excitement down in the stable yard the next day. All the pupils, including Penny, Pip, Dom, Sarah and Carlos, knew they were really lucky to be having lessons with the famous Gilly Jumpwell.

The training sessions were to be spread over three days with a mini event on the fourth day. Penny knew Patch was not very good at dressage owing to his stumpy little legs but he tried hard at the lessons. Gilly dismissed him as having very little talent for it. She had already heard of Dom's Sir Fin of course – after all, he and Dom were the current junior champions. She was terribly impressed with them. Sam and Landsman did not care for dressage much. They just wanted to gallop and jump. Gilly worked hard to convince Sam that her pony would gallop and jump even better if he was balanced from the dressage training so she practised hard. Waggit, Pip's pretty show pony, was a star performer. He pointed his toes and batted his long white eyelashes at Gilly, who quite fell in love with him.

Carlos rode Henry's Ned, who didn't think much of dressage, but Carlos rode him beautifully with his long legs and perfect seat. Gilly had dated Carlos's dad back at the 1976 Olympics in Montreal. 'I knew your father, you know,' was all she said about it to Carlos.

After the training session the ponies were hugged and rugged and put back in their stables.

That evening Gilly sat huddled by the fire in the study with Potty and three huge grey deerhounds. She was still wearing her 'teaching duvet' to keep warm as the house was freezing.

'What happened to the central heating?' asked Gilly.

Potty explained that there just was not enough money to run it and they were relying on logs and woolly jumpers to keep warm.

'Pity you haven't any drawings by Isaac Cruikshank hanging about,' shivered Gilly. 'I saw a mezzotint by him sold at auction for eight grand yesterday. It was valued at ten.'

'If only we had,' sighed the headmistress.

'I couldn't help noticing those splendid Sir Joshua Reynolds portraits in the refectory,' continued Gilly. 'They must be worth a fortune. Why don't you put them up for sale? It's the answer to your problems.'

'Oh, they do not belong to me,' said Potty Smythe. And in a way she was telling the truth.

'Penny, Penny, something has gone wrong with the plan!' Antonia and Arabella appeared in Patch's stable when Penny was mucking him out the next morning.

'Mama and Papa invited our aunt and uncle and cousin Michael over for dinner last night, together with Fern and the Montecutes, and . . . well, Michael and Fern have disappeared. We think they have eloped! We'll never have any chance of getting the old count to relinquish his picture now because Fern will not be in a position to persuade him to leave it. He will be furious with her when he finds out she's run away with Michael!'

Penny was devastated. It had seemed such a perfect plan. On the other hand, if the old count was haunting all over the place looking for the ghostly lovers, he was not going to be in his portrait. It was just a matter of finding it as quickly as possible but the cellars of Fetlocks Hall were vast, damp and dark. She was going to need some help.

After the morning's showjumping training with Gilly, in which Carlos had proved even better than his father at the sport, all five children were cleaning their tack and discussing the morning's lesson.

Penny popped her head outside the tack room to make sure the coast was clear and that no one else could hear what she was about to tell the others.

'Look,' she said, 'I've got something really important to tell you. It's got to be kept secret, but the school's in deep trouble.'

She explained about the financial mess. Everybody stood with their mouths gaping at the awful news.

'I need everyone's help. There's a famous valuable picture hidden somewhere in the cellars here and we've got to find it,' she continued. 'If Potty Smythe can sell it then Fetlocks will get at least ten thousand pounds! I have to tell you that looking for it could be dangerous and very scary.'

Sam dropped the saddle soap in the bucket with a splosh.

'Of course we'll all help!' she said and everyone agreed.

Penny showed them the catalogue from the sale.

'What a revolting-looking old man,' said Dom. 'How could anyone pay ten thousand pounds for that?'

'The original is worth much more,' said Penny. 'We'll start searching for it tonight.'

'Let's shake on it and form a league of gentlemen. We'll pledge to sacrifice all to save the school,' said Carlos in his swashbuckling way.

They did just that.

Antonia and Arabella were not going to be left out. Penny swore them into the league of gentlemen. Even though the others could not see them the twins could see the children perfectly well. They had the advantage of being able to walk through walls and see in the dark, which would be very helpful. They offered to lead Penny and her friends down into the cellars. After all, they had been playing there for hundreds of years and knew them well.

After supper they all met up in the old butler's pantry next to the door leading down into the cellars. Everyone had a torch – except for the twins who did not need one, of course! They silently beckoned to Penny, who followed them down the dark wooden steps. The rest of the league of gentlemen followed.

It was cold, dark, musty-smelling and very spooky in the cellars.

'I'm sure this place is haunted,' shivered Pip, holding on to Dom's hand.

The twins giggled and made them all freeze with fright.

'What was that?' asked Sam, her skin now covered in goosebumps.

'Oh, nothing,' said Penny, glaring at the twins who could make themselves heard if they wanted to scare people. 'Just a squeaky floorboard.'

The cellars were a series of low rooms interconnected by doors. They were full of all kinds of junk left over from the past and present inhabitants of Fetlocks Hall.

'Let's all stick together,' said Carlos, 'and search each room one by one.' Everybody thought this was a good idea.

They turned over old mattresses, bunks and junk and swings and things. Boxes of hats, racks and sacks. Old frames and window panes, stuffed bears and creaking chairs. Penny got tangled in a huge cobweb and turned round to Pip with her torch under her chin. Pip screamed and clung to Dom even harder.

They must have been down there a good hour without finding anything.

Arabella and Antonia disappeared through a wall. Penny could not follow them but fumbled in the darkness to see if she could find a secret door or opening.

Arabella's hand then came back through the wall and beckoned to Penny. It scuttled along the floor with Penny following it with the beam of her torch. Suddenly it reached up and moved an old damp spotted mirror to one side. Underneath was a large iron handle.

Penny tried to shift it but it would not budge. She called out for Carlos, who was following somewhere in the darkness behind her. Although he was much taller and stronger than Penny, he could not move the handle without Dom's help. Slowly it started to turn. With a spine-chilling creak a section of the wall slid aside. They gingerly walked into what looked like an ancient nursery. The ghostly twins were riding on an old rocking horse but to everybody except Penny it appeared to be moving on its own. They all froze. The twins were silently pointing at a small faded drawing in a frame on the wall above an old dusty fireplace. Penny walked over with her torch and wiped the cobwebs off the picture.

'Bingo!' she exclaimed. 'We've found it!'

'Hooray!' shouted Carlos.

'Whoopee!' said Sam.

'Can we get out of here now?' said Dom. 'I think Pip is going to faint.'

Carrying the picture under her arm, Penny turned round to the twins and gave them the thumbs up as the triumphant procession made their way out of the cellars to emerge in the chilly corridors of Fetlocks Hall.

Penny did not think it was too late to deliver the picture to Potty Smythe. She and Gilly were discussing old times in the study when Penny, accompanied by her friends, knocked on the door.

'We found this in the cellars,' she beamed.

Potty, dressed in a woolly hat and an old man's dressing gown, long thick socks and sheepskin slippers, could not believe her eyes! She should have told Penny the cellars were out of bounds but she forgot all about that when she saw what Penny was holding.

Everybody piled into the study and Penny put the picture down on the desk. She pulled the sale catalogue out of her pocket and smoothed it out beside the drawing. It was exactly the same picture, but the one from the cellar had some faint writing on the bottom right-hand corner.

Potty brought out her magnifying glass. Her eyes

nearly popped out as she read the name and date on the drawing.

'Isaac Cruikshank, 1775.'

It was the original!

'Perhaps you can get some central heating oil now, dear,' laughed Gilly.

The next day while Gilly was giving the children their cross-country lesson, Potty took the picture down to the sale rooms.

Mr Dodger, the antique art specialist, was very excited. He phoned his friend Mr Snailwell at Christie's, the famous art auctioneer in London. He valued it at twenty thousand pounds at least and said he had a private buyer for it immediately.

Portia Manning-Smythe could not believe her luck. The money would help enormously towards paying the school debts but it was still not nearly enough. Now all that was needed was a trip to Ireland and a chat with Scudeasy . . .

CHAPTER SIX

The Event

Little Patch loved cross-country jumping. Gilly was very pleased with Penny's performance. They were heading for a set of two downhill steps and Patch was getting a bit keen.

'Slow down, Penny,' advised Gilly. 'This kind of jump needs to be taken from a trot. Sit back, legs forward, heels down, head up, give him his reins when he pops down. Once his back feet hit the ground at the last step, pick up the reins and head for that water jump over there.'

'Better trot now, Patch,' said Penny as they cantered up to the precipice of steps.

'Oops, can't!' said Patch. 'The ground's too slippery – I can't keep my feet!'

Penny had to think quickly as they were about to tumble down the steps head first.

'*Let's Fly*!' she shouted just in time. Patch took off and flew neatly down, clearing both steps. He landed light as a feather and galloped off towards the water jump.

'*Wheee!*' he said as they leapt over the small log and down into the water.

Gilly Jumpwell stood with her mouth open. She had seen horses leap down two steps at once before but never like that. The little pony had just seemed to vanish for a second and then appear at the bottom of the steps without a jolt. Potty Smythe had been right. Penny Simms was exceptionally talented.

Waggit and Pip were next. Pip trotted neatly up to the steps and gently descended them. Pip did not sit back far enough and lost her balance on the landing.

'Head up!' shouted Gilly, but Pip had lost a stirrup. She fished for it as she was galloping on towards the water jump. Waggit did not like this kind of jump. He saw the black water coming closer and thought there was a big pony-eating monster waiting for him in its depths so he stuck his brakes on. He came to an abrupt halt at the log with his head down.

Pip sailed neatly over his head and landed in the water with a big splash. Waggit ran back to the other ponies and Dom caught him.

'Looks like she's gone surfing again,' laughed Sam.

Gilly quickly legged the soaking wet Pip up on Waggit again.

'OK,' she said, 'he's lost his confidence so let's see if he will walk gently into the water at the shallow end without a jump.'

Try as they might Waggit was not going in. He would not even follow the other ponies into the water. Gilly was getting slightly annoyed. She was not the kind of lady who gives up easily. She asked Penny if she would mind riding Waggit and having a shot at getting him into the water.

Pip agreed it would be a good idea so she swapped ponies with Penny.

Penny walked Waggit round, away from the other ponies, so she could have a word with him. He told her that his mother had got stuck in the mud on the bottom of a lake in Wales when he was a foal. He was convinced a water monster was lurking under the surface and was dragging her down. His mother was saved by the fire brigade, who got a net underneath her and lifted her out, but he had never forgotten it and was terrified of water.

'Oh, poor Waggit,' Penny said, patting his neck. 'It won't happen this time, I promise. The water is very shallow and will not even come above your pasterns. The bottom is very secure. Patch and I and all the others have been in and there is no monster there – otherwise it would have eaten us all by now.'

'I love Pip and I feel really bad about giving her a ducking each time we come to a water jump,' said Waggit, still walking around on a long rein, hanging his head.

'Come on then,' said Penny. 'Let's be brave. I'll walk in first and you can follow me. Then I'll get back on and you can carry me through. Then, once you have seen there is no water monster, let's jump in.'

Waggit agreed and was a very courageous pony. Soon they were fearlessly leaping off the log into the water at the deep end.

Gilly and the children gave Waggit a round of applause.

Penny hopped off and gave him a hug.

'See? It was easy peasy,' said Patch, nuzzling his pretty dapple grey friend.

Pip was delighted. Once back on her pony, she and Waggit were soon flying over the fallen log and galloping out of the water on the other side of the pond.

Gilly stroked Waggit's neck and thanked Penny.

There's more to this child than meets the eye, she thought to herself. *If only her dressage was up to scratch she'd be a top junior event rider. She'll be representing her country one day. I'd put my hat on that.*

The children were hacking back from the cross-country course past the main house when there was a squeal of brakes on the gravel as Potty Smythe pulled up in the Land Rover and hurtled up the steps waving a cheque.

'We're in the money, we're in the money!' she sang, dancing around the great hall with the deerhounds.

The drawing had been pronounced an original by Mr Snailwell and a cheque for twenty thousand pounds was in her hand. Now she could pay off the school overdraft and have enough money left to buy two tickets to Ireland for Penny and herself. It did not solve the whole problem. She really needed Scudeasy to win the big race. Penny was her only hope now. Could she persuade Scudeasy to win the Grand National? If so, the prize money would save Fetlocks Hall.

She called Ben's father, Willy Faloon, to tell him she and Penny would be arriving in two days' time. Then she telephoned Flanagan Airways straight away to book two tickets to Cork.

It was Gilly's last day at Fetlocks and the day of the mini event to be held within the school parkland.

Parents and teachers were invited to watch. Cleverly, Potty Smythe had sent an invitation to the Khareefs, who turned up with Matt. There were fifteen children and ponies taking part, all really excited and anxious to do well. Even Pip with her new confidence in Waggit and water jumps was bristling and raring to go.

The dressage section was first, then the show-jumping, followed by the cross-country. The scores would be calculated at the end. The winner would be the pony and rider with the lowest score.

Gilly was to judge the dressage. The children had been given a test to learn. The arena in which the test was to be performed measured twenty metres by forty metres. Around the outside of it, at specific distances apart, letters were arranged.

The ponies had to enter the arena at A and perform the test according to the instructions. It was fairly simple but included a three-loop serpentine and some lengthened strides in trot, two twenty-metre circles in canter and some loops and half circles. The ponies had to walk across the arena from M to K on a long rein to show how obedient they were. Finally they had to pick up the walk and trot again to halt neatly at X with a polite salute to the judge for the finish.

They would be given marks out of ten for each movement between the letters and added marks for how nicely the ponies went and the correct position of their riders' seats.

This seemed very complicated indeed but they had all learned and practised the test so they knew which way to go round the letters.

Carlos and Ned were drawn to go first.

Ned was a bit wobbly going up the centre line and missed C. He cantered on the wrong leg between C and M but Carlos put him right straight away. Ned was quite frustrated with it all by the end and decided he would like to go back to being a race-horse, thank you. His free walk was somewhat hurried and when Carlos picked up the reins at F he trotted off and cantered sideways down the centre line where he was supposed to be walking. He danced up and down at X instead of standing still in a perfect halt.

Penny could hear him complaining under his breath. He thought the whole thing was thoroughly stupid and never wanted to do it again!

Carlos rode him sympathetically and patiently, sitting tall and managing to look elegant whatever Ned did. Gilly gave him full marks for that but noted Ned's tense behaviour.

Pip and Waggit were next. They were used to the show ring and knew how to wow a judge. Waggit was perfectly turned out. Pip was an expert in all the tricks of her trade. She'd even put show white in his shampoo for extra whiteness, followed by condi-tioner so his lovely tail shimmered in the sunlight.

They trotted in smartly, Pip in her dark blue show jacket, velvet hat, and blonde hair in a neat bun. She smiled at Gilly, making the whole thing look light and easy. The only mistake she made was with her circles. They were not quite big enough but it was a jolly good test all the same.

Sam and Landsman were determined to conquer dressage. Sam had practised the test over and over again. Clever little Landsman now knew it by heart and was anticipating each move. The impression was of a rather hasty performance with the set movements happening slightly before they should have done at each letter.

Gilly appreciated that Sam had tried really hard but it showed too much. She made a note on the bottom of Sam's sheet not to practise the entire test on horseback so much but to learn it on foot.

Dom and Sir Fin glided in. Sir Fin was perfectly balanced, swinging his back and pointing his toes. Full of confidence, harmony, balance and rhythm, his test was just about as perfect as possible.

Penny and Patch were last to go.

'I'll be hopeless at this,' said Patch. 'I just don't have the figure for it, Pen. I don't want to let you down but I just can't stick my legs out enough to do even a respectable medium trot.'

'Trust me,' said Penny. 'We'll dance up that line between K and M and from H to F.'

Penny entered the arena in the best working trot Patch could do. She rode a very accurate test, meeting all the letters at the right time. Her straight lines were perfect. Patch was going to get full marks for obedience. When they turned up to K, where she was supposed to show some lengthened strides over X to M, Penny whispered, '*Let's Dance.*' Little Patch's legs floated over the ground like a ballerina's! Gilly Jumpwell broke her pencil. What was this amazing child doing now? Yesterday that pony was moving like a shuffling donkey. Today it was moving like a grand prix dressage horse! Unfortunately, Patch had done it too well. Instead of a medium trot he had danced an extravagant extended trot which was not required here. He got no marks for that movement at all!

After the first phase Dom was in the lead, Pip second, Penny third, Sam fourth and Carlos fifth. The last three placings went to some of the other pupils.

Carlos laughed and patted Ned. 'Not your day, Speedy Gonzales,' he said.

Penny was a bit disappointed. She thought her trot was wonderful and so it was. It was just the wrong kind of trot.

Sam knew she would catch up when it came to the cross-country section.

Pip and Dom were delighted with their marks but Dom had his doubts about Fin's speed in the showjumping and cross-country. His breeding as a German warm-blood dressage pony did not allow for fast work.

The showjumping section was next. The course was laid out in the park to the side of the drive at Fetlocks. It was a short course of ten show jumps set out in a figure of eight. Potty Smythe was the judge this time. The jumps were less than a metre high. There was only one round and the ponies had to complete the course within a set time.

Ned, expertly piloted by Carlos, made it look easy. There were no penalty points to add to his dressage score.

Pip and Waggit had two fences down, causing eight penalty points, reducing Pip's score after her dressage marks to one point above Penny and Patch.

Sam and Landsman went clear so her score did not alter.

Dom and Fin did not knock any fences down but were under the time allowed. This increased their

80

score but they were still well in the lead after such a brilliant dressage effort.

Patch skipped round clear, really enjoying himself with no time faults, to leave Penny's score unchanged.

Once all the other competitors had completed their rounds it was time to start the next phase.

The cross-country course was a permanent feature at Fetlocks Hall and everyone knew the jumps quite well. The course had been decided and flags were set up to mark the way round.

A red flag was positioned on the right of the jump and a white flag on the left. Missing out a jump, not following the course or not going between the flags would mean elimination, so it was important to walk the course and learn the way round. Henry had set it to be quite twisty.

The fences all had separate judges made up of other students and members of staff, with a score sheet to mark each rider at their specific fence. As there were twenty fences Henry appointed twenty jump judges. There was a start box for the ponies to stand in while being counted down. As soon as they left it, the clock started and the round was timed until the competitor passed the finishing line. Penalty points were given for being too fast or too slow.

These were added to your score, including other penalty points for refusals and falls. Cross-country fences are not like show jumps. They are fixed so do not fall down if the pony hits them. Fall of a pony results in elimination from the competition.

Carlos and Ned were first to go. Ned danced around in the start box while he was being counted down. Carlos looked very professional in his green sweatshirt with a yellow sideways diamond shape containing a blue spot (his Brazilian colours), and a black silk covering his crash hat. He spoke softly to the sweating Ned to try to calm him down.

As far as Ned was concerned he was under starter's orders.

'Five, four, three, two, one, GO!' shouted Henry, and Ned leapt into action.

Carlos rode him beautifully around the course but did find him a bit strong coming into a row of brush fences at the bottom of the park. Ned seemed to take off three strides in front of each one.

Carlos looked at his watch. If he did not slow Ned down somehow, he knew he would get penalty points for being too fast. He managed to get him to trot through the wooded section and hop over the stile into the water meadow. He cantered through the finish only just within the time. He did not get any penalty points.

Carlos jumped off Ned and gave him a pat. Pat Fairbrass helped to wash Ned down and remove his jumping boots. A cooler rug was thrown over him and Carlos walked him around to relax his muscles. Ned felt great. He thought it was quite like old times.

Pip and Waggit were on their way galloping towards the first fence, a small fallen log. Waggit hopped over it smartly and completed a lovely round. The water jump was no problem now. He took his rider carefully around to the finish but was a little too slow and collected two penalty points to add to Pip's score.

Cross-country riding was Sam and Landsman's speciality as they had done so much team chasing. Landsman stood still in the start box with his ears pricked. At the word 'Go' he cantered away smartly over the fences at a perfect pace. He completed the course exactly on the optimum time without any penalties. He was so fit he was not even remotely sweating. The other competitors congratulated Sam on her super round.

Dom and Sir Fin were next to go. All they had to do was get around the course now to win. It would not even matter if they picked up a few penalty points for being slow. Dom knew he had it in the bag. Perhaps that was why he did not concentrate well enough when coming through a twisty set of fences including a corner fence. He switched off and went the wrong way round a flag. He could have corrected it but he did not realise he had made a mistake! The rest of the course was easy for him. Even with the six time faults he picked up, Dom still thought he had won.

He was really mad with himself when he found out he had been eliminated from the whole competition because he'd missed a flag! Sir Fin was furious with him. He was not used to losing competitions and he knew he could have won easily on his fantastic dressage score.

Gilly came over and calmed Dom down.

'I bet you'll never do that again,' she smiled.

'Too right!' said Dom. 'I've learned my lesson not to be so sure of myself.'

That left Penny and Patch in the lead but only by one point above Pip.

There was no margin for error.

They stood in the start box, trembling with anticipation.

The flag was down and they were off.

Little Patch's legs went nineteen to the dozen until he got to the steps.

'Slow down in good time at this one,' said Penny.

Patch hopped down them but missed his footing on the landing and stumbled, tipping Penny up on to his neck and causing her to lose her stirrups. She shifted herself back into the saddle.

'Sorry,' said Patch.

'Are you OK?' asked Penny.

'Yes,' panted her friend, galloping towards the water jump, 'but you'd better hold on. Both the stirrups have come off my saddle!'

To her horror Penny realised he was right.

'You'll be safer if you grab my mane,' said Patch. 'I'll try to jump as smoothly as possible.'

Penny did as she was told as he flew over the log and splashed down into the water. She kept her head up and her heels down all the way round to a coffin, a jump consisting of three fences: a rail, then a space of three strides, then a ditch, three more strides and a jump out over an oxer or double rail with a small hedge in it.

Going over the oxer, Penny's left rein came undone. The billet attaching it to Patch's bit must have become dislodged when he stumbled at the steps. Penny had lost her steering now and the twisty section, including the corner fence where Dom had eliminated himself, was coming up!

'Just tell me where to go and hang on!' shouted Patch. 'We can win this, Pen!'

'Left here, jump the corner fence, turn sharp right and jump the sheep feeder. Go round the red flag to your right and jump the hedge into the next field. Gallop on at that hedge, Patch, because it has a ditch and drop on the other side!'

Penny had to let go of Patch's mane as she came down on the other side of the hedge because she had to get her weight back or she would fall off. She clung on to Patch with all her might, wrapping her legs around him. She leaned her upper body back and stretched her arms out and up like a pair of wings.

'Well done!' panted Patch, still going as fast as his short little legs would carry him.

'There are the finishing flags,' said Penny, looking at her watch. 'Come on, Patch, we'll only just make it. Everyone's watching so we can't fly there. It's up to you now!'

Patch was not as fit as Landsman, neither was he a former racehorse like Ned, but he galloped his little heart out for Penny and sped through the finish to the cheers of the whole school. Penny was grinning widely. With no stirrups and both hands waving madly in the air she shot past to win, her plaits streaming out behind her.

She slipped off her pony and gave him a huge hug. 'Well done, darling Patch!' she whispered into his mane.

Poor Patch was very tired and he had lost a front shoe.

'I must have pulled it off when I tripped at the steps,' he said. 'My foot hurts a bit.'

Penny picked up his near fore hoof. It was badly bruised.

'You are the bravest pony on earth,' she said as she led him limping back to the stable yard.

Matt came running over to congratulate her.

'Brilliant round, Penny,' he beamed. 'You ought to be a stunt rider!'

She thanked him but was more concerned about her pony.

Penny stroked Patch's neck. 'He's a bit lame,' she said with tears in her eyes.

The scores were being worked out in the secretary's tent to find the winner with the lowest marks. Henry pinned the results to the scoreboard with the winners' names underlined to eighth place.

Everyone crowded around for the prize-giving.

'And the overall winner is . . . Penny Simms with Patchwork with 77 points,' said Gilly Jumpwell, holding a large silver cup and a red rosette. 'Where are you, Penny?'

The crowd looked round but Penny was nowhere to be seen.

She had sneaked off to the secret hiding place between the two stone unicorns on the front steps of Fetlocks Hall to fetch the little vial of Unicorn Tears King Valentine Silverwings had given her. Back in Patch's stable she was busy dabbing some of the silver liquid on to Patch's foot.

It healed instantly.

'You are a star,' said Patch, nuzzling her ear.

CHAPTER SEVEN

A Chat with Scudeasy

The whole school lined up in the great hall to say goodbye to Gilly Jumpwell. Pip presented her with a large bouquet of flowers from everybody to say thank you for the lessons, her help and encouragement. Mr and Mrs Khareef were especially impressed with the whole event.

'The children have such wonderful team spirit,'

said Mr Khareef, shaking her hand.

'There has always been a tradition of competitive but friendly and helpful students at Fetlocks,' said Gilly. 'That counts for a lot in my book.'

Gilly descended the steps with Potty Smythe.

'You were right about the little Simms girl,' she said. 'She is definitely one to watch. Not only does she ride extremely well but she also seems to have some magical communication with ponies. She is quite exceptional.'

The headmistress agreed. She was secretly hoping Penny could work some magic on the reluctant Scudeasy during their impending trip to Ireland.

Gilly swished away in the blue sports car. She was not intending to go straight home quite yet. She was heading towards Dorchester for dinner with Anthony Redcheek first!

Penny and Potty Smythe were due to fly out to Cork the next day.

Penny had packed her tatty little leather suitcase and was saying goodbye to Patch. His foot cured, he was having a few days off as well to recover from the event.

She assured him she would be all right on the plane.

'We could have flown there ourselves,' he sighed, not wanting to be left out.

Dressed in her school uniform, Penny hurried behind the headmistress through the departure hall at the airport. They only had hand luggage so it meant travelling was easier.

'What a nice little girl,' said the pretty air hostess as she checked Penny's seat belt. 'Is this the first time you've ever flown?'

'Er, not exactly,' said Penny. She could hardly explain that this was her first trip in an aircraft and that her only experience of flying was on ponies!

She thought it very tiresome that the aircraft had to taxi such a long way before it lifted off. Patch just ascended neatly like an angel vertically from the ground.

From the sky Ireland looked very much like England. They had left in bright sunshine only to land at Cork in a thick mist of light rain.

Penny ran up to Ben, who was waiting for them at the airport. He picked her up and whirled her around.

'Now what's all this I hear about you being an event star?' he laughed.

'And all with no stirrups and no reins!' added Potty Smythe.

Soon they were rumbling down the road in the Faloons' pickup truck towards the Ballywater Valley, where Willy Faloon had his racing yard. They turned up a drive and stopped before some huge wooden gates. Ben tapped out a code on the number pad on one of the brick pillars. The gates opened and closed behind them.

'Tight security,' he said, pulling up outside the office.

Willy Faloon was a small stocky man with a red face and a shock of black hair going silver in places. He had darting blue eyes under very thick black eyebrows. Penny thought he looked like a small plump eagle. He did not seem to have a neck but his head swivelled round, bird-like, from his telephone call to give them a crooked toothy smile as they came in.

'Ya, ya, ya, bye bye now, bye bye now, bye bye now,' he spluttered into the phone in his soft Cork accent.

'Potty Smythe!' he grinned. 'Now it's lovely to see you so. And this would be the little wonder I've been hearing all about. Jumps hedges with no reins and no stirrups. Sure I'd give her a job any time.'

He stood up and shook Penny by the hand.

'You are still the old rascal you always were, Willy,' laughed Potty.

'Well, there's more snow on the roof,' said Willy Faloon, rubbing a paw-like hand through his thick greying hair.

Willy's yard was vast and very modern.

One hundred and fifty racehorses lived under one roof. The place was like a huge aircraft hangar. It had rubber floors and lines of roomy internal loose boxes. The solarium, isolation boxes for visiting horses, a horse walker (or carousel for exercising the racehorses), tack room, rug room, feed room and hay barn were all in beautiful order. The lean, mus-cled racehorses all chomped away at their hay nets. They had large bright shiny eyes and glistening coats and were in the peak of fitness.

Penny loved it. They all shouted 'Hello there' in Equalese with Irish accents as she walked in.

'Very pleased to meet you all,' said Penny. 'Which one of you is Scudeasy?'

'Here I am so,' said a very tall bay horse with a long nose.

Penny had never seen such a big horse before. He must be eighteen hands high. She thought all thoroughbreds were small and light with pretty heads. Scudeasy was none of these things. She walked over to him and gave his nose a rub.

'Now you're a nice little girl, so you are,' he said. 'And where did you learn to speak Equalese like that? Sure it's very handy to be able to talk to a human being.'

'The unicorns gave me the gift,' said Penny. 'I'm a Unicorn Princess.'

'Oh, that'd explain it then. We don't see unicorns much here. We have our own version though.'

Penny was intrigued to know what an Irish unicorn looked like. Scudeasy explained they were much smaller, bright green and ate shamrocks.

'Ballycorns,' he said. 'Charming little t'ings.'

Penny wondered if she would be lucky enough to ever see one.

'Oh, they're not shy,' continued Scudeasy. 'They're always carousing and singing and playing practical jokes on each other. They drink a golden elixir of buttercup dew. It makes them quite tipsy sometimes, especially on St Patrick's Day. They've been known to fly backwards. I've never seen one myself though.'

'Don't believe a word of it,' laughed a chestnut horse in the next stable. 'He's kissed the Blarney Stone so many times his lips have no skin left on them. Ballycorns indeed! Sure there's no such thing!'

'Shut your ugly gob, Seamus O'Driscol,' said Scudeasy with his teeth bared and his ears back.

'Sure I'll kick you hard next time you try to bump me on the track!'

Portia Manning-Smythe was watching Penny from the other side of the building. She could not hear any of this conversation, of course, but she could see some sort of communication was going on.

The Faloons lived in a one-storey cottage adjacent to the internal yard. Kathleen Faloon, Ben's mother, made them very welcome. They were a large family but only Ben's younger brother, Tom, still lived at home. He worked on the yard with his father and already had his jockey licence. Patsy and Jack, Ben's older brothers, were bloodstock agents in the Curragh up in Kildare. They bought and sold racehorses in the centre of the Irish racing world. Ben's two sisters were married with small children of their own. The younger one was in Hong Kong working at the Hong Kong Jockey Club.

The cottage was warm and cosy with a peat fire burning in the grate. The walls were covered with photographs of past winners, certificates, press cuttings and rosettes. There was a glass cabinet packed with large silver trophies. Two liver and white springer spaniels lay on either side of the fire in wicker baskets. They rushed up, wagging their tails, as soon as their owners and guests came into the room.

Kathleen had done them proud. She'd boiled them a 'bacon' or large hunk of gammon. There were boiled potatoes and colcannon, a kind of cabbage, potato and onion mash. Steamed suet pudding with sultanas called a 'spotted dick' doused with thick creamy custard followed.

'Just the thing for a cold wet night in Cork!' she said as she dished it all up on the kitchen table.

Penny decided Ireland was the best place in the world!

As she started on her pudding, she asked if she could see Scudeasy run tomorrow.

'We'll run the old horse up the training gallops for you on his tod,' said Ben, 'and then run him with the pack. You'll see what he does.'

'He does nothing!' said Willy, his mouth full of pudding. 'He's as useless as a lame donkey and if it wasn't for Ben liking the old fellow so, he'd have been down the kennels by now.'

What he meant was that Scudeasy would have been shot and boiled up for the Dunmarrow hounds' dinner!

'There must be a reason for his odd behaviour,' said Potty Smythe, tucking into the spotted dick. 'He was a good enough horse in his day. He won the Guineas and the Irish Grand National.'

'He's a fantastic horse,' said Ben, 'but I've tried everything I know. Let's hope you two experts can help him now that you're here. You may be the only chance of saving him!'

Penny had no time to lose. She planned to have a chat with Scudeasy the next day.

Kathleen had put Potty Smythe in the only spare bedroom. Penny was to curl up on the sofa in a mauve duvet in front of the fire for the night with the spaniels and a large black cat called Orla. The cat slept on Penny's chest. She woke at six in the morning to a loud purring and two bright green eyes staring into hers.

Ben and Willy had been on the yard since 5 a.m. and fed the horses. The first lot were to be out on the gallops by eight. Penny wondered when racehorse people ever got any sleep. They always had very early mornings and very late nights.

They came in for breakfast at six thirty. Kathleen had the table groaning again with bacon rashers, fried eggs, tomatoes, sausages, fried bread and baked beans. Huge steaming mugs of tea were poured from a teapot clad in a tea cosy the shape of a ballerina. After breakfast, Willy drove them up the hill to the top of the gallops. It was a damp start to the day. Somewhere below them in the mist Ben had

Scudeasy bouncing and ready to go.

Willy sounded the car's horn as a signal for Ben to start. The great horse leapt into action and pounded his way up the hill at a very impressive speed. He emerged out of the mist, breathing clouds of steam like a huge dragon, and pulled up in front of the group of spectators.

'That was amazing!' said Penny to Scudeasy when he arrived at the top of the hill. 'You must be the fastest horse on earth!'

'No,' breathed the big ugly horse, 'that was my grandfather, Secretariat.'

Ben gave his horse a pat and trotted back to the start where he now joined the other horses for his next run.

Willy looked at his stopwatch and sounded the horn again. Moments later a pack of super-fit race-horses appeared at full gallop. Scudeasy was nowhere to be seen. They pulled up and the other jockeys walked their horses in circles to keep them warm. Fifteen minutes later Scudeasy turned up at a trot.

Ben was exhausted. He'd had to kick Scudeasy for a mile and a half to get him to finish the course. He trotted the horse over to Penny, handed her the reins and flopped down on his back in the wet grass.

'What went wrong, Scudeasy?' asked Penny. 'You could have beaten them with both front hoofs tied behind your back.'

'I don't like the other horses,' he said. 'They are rude and careless. Their jockeys are no better. I was once badly bumped by one of them, causing me to fall at a fence in the Blantyre Cup. I hurt my back badly. My owners couldn't see anything wrong with me so they kept me in training. It was terribly painful. For the love of Finn MacCool, I'm not racing again!'

With that he did a squeal and a buck and trotted off after the rest of the racehorses. Penny knew there was obviously nothing wrong with his back now if he could behave like that.

'He should be down the kennels,' mumbled Willy Faloon.

Penny had a tough job here. Scudeasy was obviously quite a character. By his breeding he was racehorse aristocracy and used to having his own way. They were flying home the next day so she had little time to help him with his problem.

She sat in his stable all afternoon. She explained about Fetlocks Hall and the money problems that would lead to it being closed down and the ponies sold. He pricked up his ears when she told him the incredible story of how she found the picture of

Count Blackdrax and raised some money to save the school, but it was not enough. What they needed now was for Scudeasy to win the Grand National. The prize money, which Ben had generously decided to give to Potty, would save Fetlocks from being closed down and the ponies from being sold.

The horse said nothing. He just munched his hay net.

'Please, Scudeasy,' Penny pleaded. 'You are our only hope. We know you can do it!'

Still he ignored her. She had one card left to play. It was a dirty one but her only hope with this stubborn horse.

'Willy Faloon wants you sent to the kennels,' she whispered. 'It's only Ben who's keeping you alive. You owe him your life. You owe it to him to try.'

Scudeasy nearly choked on his hay. He went into a fit of coughing. He shot Penny a cold stare down his long nose.

'And if they bring Ben and me down in that, the most dangerous of all horse races, we could both be killed!' he snorted.

Penny saw his point. Many horses and jockeys had been killed or injured in the Grand National over the years. Scudeasy was trying to protect Ben as well. She thought for a moment. There had to be a way of persuading him to take a chance.

'What if I can make it safe for you to run in some way?'

'Impossible,' said the great horse. 'The only way you can do that is to make it a one-horse race. That means I'd be the only one running. Foinavon did it with John Buckingham in 1967.'

Now it was Penny's turn to prick up her ears.

'Will you agree if I can make sure you and Ben come to no harm?'

Scudeasy lowered his big head and nuzzled Penny on the nose.

'I'll think about it so,' he said. 'Come back at teatime and I'll let you know my answer.'

'Oh, thank you, thank you, you lovely horse,' cried Penny, throwing her arms round his neck. 'I'll be back!'

That evening Penny took Scudeasy his evening feed. He was still undecided about running the race.

She stroked his glossy neck as he munched away. Not only was she going to have to be diplomatic with this aristocrat of the turf but she would have to pull rank as well.

'Don't worry, sir,' she said. 'After all, I am a Unicorn Princess and I can make extraordinary things happen. I promise to make it safe for you and Ben. I'll make you the most famous Grand National winner ever.'

'I like the sound of that,' said Scudeasy. 'Let's give it a try.'

'Trust me!' said Penny, giving him a hug.

CHAPTER EIGHT

Lady Fitznicely's
Knickers

Penny returned to the house, where Potty Smythe was waiting to hear the results of her chat with Scudeasy.

'Well, Penny, how did you get on?' asked the headmistress.

Penny told Potty Smythe about the horse's problem and the agreement they had made.

Potty Smythe looked downcast. 'It's going to be impossible to make the Grand National a safe race,' she sighed. 'It's not worth even taking him over to Liverpool for it.'

Penny needed some time to think and a great deal of luck. She asked Potty Smythe exactly what had happened in 1967 when Foinavon won the National.

'Foinavon was a total outsider,' said Potty. 'He was miles behind the others. When it came to the twenty-third fence some loose horses stopped, ran across it and brought the whole field to a stop. Foinavon's jockey could see this pile-up way in front of him and steered him through the other horses to jump the fence. By the time they had all remounted and got going he had won the race.'

'What made them stop?' asked Penny.

'No one knows,' said Potty Smythe. 'Maybe they saw a ghost!'

Penny looked quizzical and crossed her arms.

'Maybe they did,' she said.

Penny was looking forward to getting back to Fetlocks Hall and Patch but she did not want to leave Ireland either. Kathleen packed them up some soda bread sandwiches and a flask of tea. She gave Penny a huge hug and told Potty to bring her little angel back soon. On Penny's recommendation Potty Smythe handed over Scudeasy's entry fee for the Grand National. She had kept enough back from the sale of Count Blackdrax's portrait. Most of it had gone towards paying off the school's bank overdraft. It was now cleared but would have to be run up again as the school had to survive for the next few weeks. If Scudeasy did not win the National, Fetlocks would be in deep trouble.

They left Willy filling in entry forms in the office and Ben drove them to the airport. He thanked her for putting up the money.

'He has not the remotest chance of winning,' said Ben, who had no idea about Penny's deal with Scudeasy, 'but he's the safest and best jumper. He can jump those fences from a trot.'

'Don't give up so easily,' said Penny. 'He who dares wins. Just keep him super-fit for the race.

Back at Fetlocks nothing had changed except that the school was a great deal warmer. The head-mistress had also kept some of the picture money to buy some central heating oil.

A sleet storm was blowing in the park as Penny and Potty Smythe battled their way through the wind to the front doors. Penny went down to see Patch and the ponies straight away.

Patch was feeling livelier now after his rest and trotted up to his door to greet Penny. She filled him in on the news from Ireland.

'Are ponies frightened of ghosts?' she asked him.

'Only the really scary ones,' he said. 'The Fitznicelys and the de Parrotts are fine. I didn't like the look of Count Blackdrax though. I hope he never comes here again.'

'He won't,' answered Penny. 'His picture has been sold.'

In fact Count Blackdrax was quite pleased that his picture had been moved. Mr Snailwell had kept it himself instead of selling it to the client he had promised it to. He hung it in the hall of his smart house in London. He wished he hadn't because the horrible old count found his new haunting place very convenient for his tailor in nearby Savile Row and for his club, both frequent haunts of his. He dropped in regularly on Mr Snailwell and now hung out in his portrait, treating it as his new London home and scaring the wits out of the family.

Penny put an extra rug on Patch as it was bitterly cold outside in his stable. Then she made her way back to the main house.

The Fitznicelys were also delighted the old count had moved but they were concerned that nobody had heard from Michael de Parrott and Fern Montecute. They had simply disappeared.

'We ghosts have a habit of doing that and then popping up in the most unexpected places,' said Lady Sarah, arranging a vase of daffodils in the hall. 'I remember our old gardener, Abel Smith. He was cutting the topiary in the grounds one day and totally disappeared. Apparently, he suddenly appeared in 1967 cutting a hedge which happened to be a jump in that year's Grand National. He spooked the horses so badly they all stopped. He had disappeared by the time the last horse came along. It went on to win the race.'

Maybe that's what caused the 1967 pile-up, thought Penny.

'Dear Sir Walter was a great racegoer,' continued Lady Sarah. 'In fact his friend, the Duke of Devonshire, invented racehorse breeding as you know it today. The Duke always said horses could see ghosts. I remember during a race at Newmarket in 1722, shortly after I married Sir Walter, he had a horse running called Flying Childers. He was convinced the horse could see spirits so he decided to run him in blinkers. We had none on the course at the time so I offered to help by supplying my drawers to make him a pair. The horse won the race and the Duke ran him in them until he retired. He was certain they were ghost-proof. More likely they prevented Childers from seeing the horses on either side of him. My pantaloon blinkers made him feel much safer and less at risk of being harmed by the other runners. Flying Childers lived to be one of the greatest winners of the turf and all through wearing my drawers!'

Penny's mind was racing too.

If Scudeasy could wear such blinkers, he too would not be able to see the other horses in the race. He would feel super-safe!

Penny explained the situation to Lady Sarah, who said she still had the Ghostly Blinkers. The Duke had given them back to her when Flying Childers retired to stud. In fact she had them on at this very moment. She always wore them for good luck.

Penny asked Lady Sarah if she might borrow them. She agreed and whipped them off straight through her gown.

Penny stuffed them into her pocket and thanked her profusely.

After her chemistry lesson with Professor Greengas Penny paid a visit to the headmistress's study and told Potty Smythe of her plan.

'Whatever happens Scudeasy must go to Aintree. I really believe he has a chance of saving himself,' Penny said.

It only remained to persuade Scudeasy to wear the blinkers.

Over the next few weeks Potty Smythe phoned Ben and Willy Faloon regularly to check on Scudeasy's progress. It was essential he be sound and fit to run.

The twins had some ghostly gossip for Penny. Fern Montecute and Michael de Parrott had reappeared at Templecombe. They had got married secretly in Brighton and Michael had run up debts all over the place. They were now penniless and their parents were so furious they refused to help. To make matters worse Count Blackdrax had challenged Michael to a duel. Although Michael was much younger than the old count he was no swordsman. The count, however, was a ruthless swordsman and had won many a duel.

Penny decided a visit to Templecombe was a good idea so she flew Patch over there that night.

Sir Edwin and Lucy de Parrott, the living descendants of the de Parrott family, were reading newspapers by the fire in the drawing room. They had no idea that their ghostly ancestors were having a row in the same room.

'I am simply not paying these!' raged Sir Rupert, throwing a stack of bills into the air. 'You are a wastrel and a rascal, Michael, and you, young lady, have done a very stupid thing in marrying him. Your own parents have disowned and disinherited you and until *you*, Michael, pay your own debts, I am doing the same!'

Fern, clinging to Michael's hand, burst into tears.

'Please, Father,' pleaded Michael, 'we have nowhere to go. I will probably be killed by the count and dearest Fern widowed. Then he will marry her and make her life a misery.'

Lady Beatrice stood up and clasped her hands. She pleaded with her husband to show some compassion for their son and daughter-in-law but it only seemed to make him angrier.

'Michael,' he blustered, 'you are as stupid as you are a hopeless spendthrift. You are a ghost and have been dead for hundreds of years. So how, pray, can Count Blackdrax kill you at all?'

Michael and Fern were thrown out of the house and told never to haunt it again.

Penny, circling over the lawn, spotted them floating towards the folly by the lake. They sat inside it, looking very sad. Fern was weeping on Michael's shoulder. Penny landed Patch and led him over to the building. Michael explained everything. He was most worried about the duel.

'Father's right – ghosts can't really get killed or die twice,' said Michael, 'but if I have to duel with the count and he does mortally wound me I will evaporate. It makes haunting a second time really difficult. I may never see Fern again.'

'Have you any money at all?' said Penny.

'Just one guinea,' sobbed Fern.

'Can you choose a place and time for the duel?' asked Penny.

'Yes,' answered Michael. 'As the one who is being challenged I choose the weapons and a time and place.'

'Then I can help,' said Penny, 'if you make it the same day and time as the Grand National. Everyone will be there in case of . . . well . . . an *accident*.'

Fern sobbed even louder.

Penny was planning to take her silver vial of Unicorn Tears with her to the race just in case Scudeasy was hurt before the start. It might even come in handy if Michael got wounded during the duel. She also intended to bring Queen Starlight's

Horn. Its music was supposed to calm wild beasts so it might work on the beastly old count and reduce his duelling powers. She was not sure if her magic gifts would have any effect on ghosts but it was worth a try.

She flew Patch back to Fetlocks, hoping all her plans for the race day would work.

CHAPTER NINE

The Grand National

Portia Manning-Smythe had booked a bus to take some of the children to Aintree to watch the big race. Mrs Honeybun made an enormous packed lunch for thirty children and six members of staff.

Pat Fairbrass was left behind to do the yard so Henry could go with the children. This gave her another opportunity to spend some time with Peter Fixcannon, who was coming along as well for a day out.

It was a long way from Dorset to Liverpool so they

had to set off very early in the morning. Nevertheless, the whole busload of children were wide awake and singing and hooting. Henry was going to share the driving with Potty and Peter so they would not get too tired.

Penny had never been racing before and was terribly excited. She was hoping against hope that the Ghostly Blinkers plot would work. Bunty Bevan was coming up to watch the race and bringing Penny's family with her. Penny was dying to see them all but had her mind on more important things. She checked Lady Fitznicely's bloomers were safely stuffed in her blazer pocket. They were invisible to humans but not to horses. Hopefully Scudeasy would have no objection to wearing them on his head as blinkers. The vial of Unicorn Tears was safely stowed in the other pocket and Queen Starlight's Horn was tucked between her blazer buttons just in case.

There was a big traffic jam going into Aintree. Penny was getting nervous. It was vital she get to Scudeasy on time before the race. Security was very tight at the racecourse and somehow she had to reach the horse and fit the blinkers on him. Willy Faloon had sent two exclusive passes to the stable area but they had little time to find it.

Once parked, Potty and Penny ran through the massive crowds to find Willy, who directed them on his mobile phone, at the entrance to the yard.

Ben had weighed in and was saddling up Scudeasy in his stable when they arrived.

'You took your time, little girl,' said Scudeasy to Penny. 'I'm telling you I am not racing unless you have made this safe for Ben and myself.'

Penny swallowed hard. 'Trust me, Scudeasy. Now just put your head down and close your eyes.'

She whipped the blinkers out of her pocket and fixed them on to his head.

They looked really funny. His long nose was pointing out of the waistband and his ears poked out of the frilly pink leg holes. Two extra holes had been cut for his eyes. Penny, who was the only one who could see this apparition, stifled a laugh.

'Blinkers?' said Scudeasy. 'I have never run in blinkers.'

'These are very special ones,' Penny assured him, hoping he would not catch a glimpse of himself in them anywhere. If he knew he was really wearing a pair of bloomers on his head he would surely have chucked them off or refused to go out of his stable. Scudeasy was a very aristocratic thoroughbred and would not have been seen dead wearing ladies' underwear!

He was led out to the paddock looking lean and fit. He appeared to be very cool and confident in his Ghostly Blinkers. They seemed to be having the right effect.

The racecourse was buzzing. Penny had never seen so many people and ghosts all in one place. She was glad to see the Fitznicelys had made it. They were seated in the royal box alongside the Montecute and de Parrott families. She also noticed a girl in a grey hooded cloak. When the girl turned round she saw it was Fern in disguise. She looked thin and pale, even for a ghost.

'Oh, dearest Penny,' she said tearfully, 'we did as you suggested and the duel is arranged for this afternoon after the race. But Michael has to choose the weapons and he does not know anything about swords or pistols or that kind of thing!'

'Tell him to choose some that won't hurt, like feather pillows or custard pies,' said Penny. 'That will stall the count until I have time to help later.'

Fern looked rather confused for a moment but her face lit up as Penny's cunning plan dawned on her. She trotted off with her one guinea to buy some pies from the racecourse market.

Penny did not want to sound unconcerned but she had other things on her mind right now.

Back in the paddock the other horses were looking at Scudeasy's blinkers and laughing. She hoped he hadn't heard them and become suspicious of the bloomers on his head. There was no time to change his mind now about running because the jockeys were coming out to mount up and ride down to the start!

Penny and Portia Manning-Smythe's special tickets allowed them into the paddock with the horses, their owners, trainers and jockeys.

Willy had two other horses running in the race and was not concerned about Scudeasy. He thought it was a waste of time bringing him anyway.

Potty Smythe legged Ben up on to the big horse as Penny held the reins.

The headmistress reassured him everything would be OK and wished him the best of luck.

'You are going to win this,' Penny whispered to Scudeasy. 'Go out and scare them. You know you are the best horse in the race.'

Scudeasy tossed his long head and bounced sideways as she led him out of the paddock and on to the famous racecourse.

'Just stay in the lead,' said Penny, unclipping the leading rein. 'Good luck both of you!'

* * *

The crowd cheered as the runners and riders went down to the start.

The other horses were milling around nervously, waiting for starter's orders. All except Scudeasy, who was standing poised like an arrow.

The starter's flag was up, lowered, and they were off.

The big horse flew into action, eating up the ground with his long strides. He went straight into the lead, setting a blistering pace.

One by one he glided over the huge fences, making them look small.

By the time they reached the Canal Turn there were only twenty horses left in the race but they were far behind. Others had fallen or tipped their jockeys off. Ben and Scudeasy were cruising. He took Valentine's Brook in a huge bound and landed safely on the other side.

The crowd were making a deafening din, encouraging the horses on. Penny and the others were watching from the grandstand. She crossed her fingers in the pockets of her school blazer. The only danger was that Scudeasy would become too confident, make a mistake and fall.

But by the second time round, four of the other horses seemed to be catching up. One of them was the favourite, Diamond Blade. Across the Melling

Road he was definitely gaining speed. They were coming up for their second attempt at Becher's Brook.

Penny had her heart in her mouth. Ben just had to keep Scudeasy's long nose in front or he would hear Diamond Blade coming up behind him and slow down for fear he might get hurt.

Ben glanced back at the other horse, his goggles smeared with mud.

They were coming to the last fence now. He could not make a mistake. Diamond Blade was on Scudeasy's tail. He gave a massive leap and landed neck and neck with him.

Penny could not bear to look – surely it was all over now? Scudeasy must have seen him!

But the crowd was going mad! Scudeasy knew he was winning and he was loving every minute of it. The Ghostly Blinkers were preventing him from seeing the other horse at his side but he knew it was there. He forgot his fear – the old Scudeasy was back! He put his head down, lowered his pasterns and strode on to win the Grand National!

The Fetlocks Hall crew went crazy! Whooping and cheering, the children tossed their hats into the air.

Portia Manning-Smythe hugged Penny, Willy Faloon hugged Portia Manning-Smythe.

The race was won. Fetlocks Hall was saved and so was the remarkable Scudeasy!

Ben rode him into the winner's enclosure, led by Penny. She pulled the blinkers over his ears and stuffed them back in her pocket.

Scudeasy, covered in sweat and breathing hard, put his big red nostrils to her ear.

'Well,' he breathed, 'now aren't you a clever little girl indeed, Princess Penny.'

'You are my hero,' she said, stroking his nose.

Penny's parents, Oliver and her sisters waved at her from the crowd. Mr Simms passed Ollie over the fence to Willy Faloon, who hoisted him up on to Scudeasy's back.

'Ollie ride racehorses!' he giggled.

Ben was weighed in again and they all marched off to the prize-giving to collect the huge trophy and take it back to Ireland. There was also an enormous cheque for the prize money which Ben handed over to Potty Smythe, who could not thank him enough. She gave him a big hug and the cheque a big kiss. She danced around, waving it above her head. It was enough to pay off all the school's debts. Fetlocks was now safe and so were its ponies.

The cameras flashed and the press crowded in.

The Fetlocks Hall children screamed, whistled and sent up a joyous but ear-piercing view holla.

'*WHOOOOEEEEEEH!*' they screamed.

Pip, Dom, Carlos and Sam came over to give Scudeasy a pat and help wash the sweat out of his coat, dry him and bandage his legs with ice packs.

'Potty Smythe's had double luck today,' said Sam as she sponged him down. 'Matt just texted me. His parents were so impressed with our one-day event and what Gilly said about us that they have decided to send him to Fetlocks Hall!'

'That's so cool,' said Penny. 'I'm sure he'll sail through the entrance exam.'

'And that was fantastic Unicorn Princess work today. Well done, Penny,' came two familiar voices.

Arabella and Antonia Fitznicely floated up and hovered over the busy children.

'You will never guess what else has happened,' giggled Antonia. 'Michael de Parrott was just lining up the custard tarts for the duel when one of his friends arrived with some wonderful news. He has become fantastically rich because one of the daft inventions he invested in has turned out not to be so silly after all! Alexander Cummings, his best chum, has invented the first flushing toilet (it being 1775 in our past time). It is a roaring success. No need for chamber pots any more. Much nicer for the poor servants who had to empty them. Fern has persuaded him to give some of his money to her parents to keep Montecute Hall going. The de Parrotts are delighted with Michael for once and they've told the old count to stuff his silly duel and get lost!'

Penny thought she would burst with laughter.

'And what's the matter with you, young lady?' said Ben, who of course could not see or hear any of this conversation.

'Oh, it's all this good news,' said Penny.

Willy Faloon came over, carrying the huge trophy.

'I was so wrong about that horse of yours, son,' he said, 'but I've always been right about you. What about handing in your notice at the school and staying at home with us in the Ballywater Valley? You've a brilliant racing career ahead of you.'

Penny looked anxiously at Ben, who took her hand and squeezed it.

'Not just yet, Da,' he said grinning down at her, his face splattered with mud. 'There's something a bit special about Fetlocks Hall. I don't think I want to work anywhere else. There's no other place quite like it!'

THE END (for the time being)